ON THE WARPATH

Gerald Hammond titles available from
Severn House Large Print

Cold in the Heads
The Dirty Dollar
Down the Garden Path
The Hitch
The Snatch

ON THE WARPATH

Gerald Hammond

Severn House Large Print
London & New York

This first large print edition published in Great Britain 2007 by
SEVERN HOUSE LARGE PRINT BOOKS LTD of
9-15 High Street, Sutton, Surrey, SM1 1DF.
First world regular print edition published 2006 by
Severn House Publishers, London and New York.
This first large print edition published in the USA 2007 by
SEVERN HOUSE PUBLISHERS INC., of
595 Madison Avenue, New York, NY 10022.

British Library Cataloguing in Publication Data

Hammond, Gerald, 1926-
  On the warpath. - Large print ed.
  1. Swindlers and swindling - Fiction 2. Grandparent and
  child - Fiction 3. Revenge - Fiction 4. France - Fiction
  5. Large type books
  I. Title
  823.9'14[F]

  ISBN-13: 978-0-7278-7606-5

Printed and bound in Great Britain by
MPG Books Ltd, Bodmin, Cornwall.

This story contains some wholly fictitious incidents from the French Resistance. These are not intended to impugn in any way the very gallant fighters who served in it.

I have to thank my good friend Abigail Gordon and my longstanding friend, her husband Peter. They made us welcome in their Dordogne home and kept me more or less straight on matters of language, geography and history.

The minds of some people may go blank in an emergency. Others find that time passes too quickly for thought. But Helen was no stranger to emergencies. During a long and successful career in TV journalism she had faced up to extreme danger from warfare, earthquakes, volcanoes, terrorists and jealous lovers. She had survived plane and car crashes. If all the blood that she had lost in these various incidents had been spilled on a single occasion, she could not possibly have survived. That she had survived at all was down, in part, to luck but mostly to quickness of mind and unshakeable courage.

With danger now coming at her from within and without, even her quick mind was not quick enough to review her long life. But within that dire moment came awareness of who she had been and might well cease to be. It was all there, the experiences that had made her what she was. It was her distilled essence, there and gone in the blink of an eye.

One

Call her what you will – Granny, Nan, Nana or Hey you!, we all have an image in mind of the stereotypical grandmother. She is well on in years, or even of incredible antiquity if we ourselves are young. She is small, probably rather round, with silver hair, an endearing expression and pockets full of sweets. She may smell of mothballs. She has devoted her life to raising children and spoiling grandchildren. Ask her to attempt anything physical and she will probably fall on her face.

Outwardly, Helen would have seemed to conform to that stereotype. On closer observation, the new acquaintance might have noticed some features differing from those usually found in grandmothers. An active working life and a retirement largely spent gardening and exercising a pack of spaniels had allowed her to retain a youthful spring in her step and a tidy figure very little run to seed. Her cheeks were striated with fine wrinkles but they were still pink. Her normal voice was soft and she knew how to play the plaintive old lady well enough to fool any policeman or parking warden, but importunate door-to-door salesmen who thought that they had found a soft touch she could reduce to quivering jelly by means of a raised voice and a turn of phrase that was both vivid and corrosive.

Helen had been born in France of an English mother. Her father, Philippe Mercier, was a handsome Frenchman from the Dordogne. He was neat and well built and his manner of courtship was both romantic and respectful – a combination that very few Englishmen had achieved. He had been visiting England on a consultancy job on behalf of his parent firm when he met and fell for Pauline, the attractive daughter of a client. After a cautious enquiry to assure herself that he did not already have a wife in France, Pauline returned his affection and married him. When his work in England was finished, he carried his bride back to France, thereby missing the worst effects of the recession that had followed the General Strike.

They were happy in France, while it lasted. That is to say, until Philippe caught an infection. In those pre-penicillin days, an infection could be very serious.

'Will you go back to England?' Philippe asked faintly. He spoke in English. Pauline's French was still not better than 'getting by'.

'You'll get better,' she said.

Philippe had his doubts but he said, 'Suppose that I did not.'

'No. I don't think so.'

'I will not leave you well provided for.'

'Then don't go.'

He patted her hand and slipped into a deep sleep from which he failed to awake.

Helen was born shortly afterwards.

Pauline loved France. Additionally, she had parted acrimoniously with her family (who had been determined that she should not marry any damn foreigner and especially not a Frenchman). Without Philippe to interpret for her, her French improved rapidly. Philippe had not been a wealthy man but his widow's pension, supplemented by teaching English three days a week at a local school, kept body and soul together. They paid only a peppercorn rent for a small but comfortable cottage built in the golden local stone. They were surrounded by beautiful countryside. The nearby village, well within cycling distance, could supply most of their needs; for anything else there was a small town only a bus ride away, where a market once a week could provide whatever the shops could not. If Pauline missed her Philippe, her daughter at least partially filled the gap.

Their existence was almost idyllic, until the Germans came.

Even then, superficially life seemed little changed at first. A thousand new regulations were obeyed or ignored, at first, according to how the locals felt inclined. They were away from the coast and too far south to bear the brunt of the occupation. Helen, and apparently her mother, lived quietly and seemed to ignore the censorship of news, the grey uniforms and the guns. The nearest bomb fell many miles away. Helen spoke perfect French but was taught English and she played with Jules Petiot, the son of a nearby farmer. Jules was a year and a bit older than Helen, a sturdy boy with dark hair, a thin face and a happy laugh. When Pauline was away, which began to happen more often, Helen was left in the care of Jules's mother. Pauline explained that she was teaching at evening classes in the town.

It was not to last. After nearly two years, the Germans came and took Helen's mother away. Madame Petiot, puffing slightly because she was putting on weight in spite of the war, came to call. 'Little one,' she said, 'I have been delegated to break the news. Did you know that your mother worked for the Resistance?'

'I guessed it,' Helen said. 'Tell me quickly what has happened.'

'We only have rumours and guesswork but

11

we know that she did not talk. It seems that she has been shot.'

Helen sat quietly, looking at the cottage wall. She never shed a tear, although tears were not far away.

Helen and her mother had been well liked. What was more, a little money and a small pension came with her. Madame Petiot opened her arms and her door and took Helen in. As the war dragged on, they settled again into quiet, rural life, if less placid than before, until Helen was seventeen. She and Jules still played together, but their games were not always such as her mother would have approved. Jules, in particular, pleaded constantly to be allowed to take that ultimate step into paradise and Helen, though her fondness for him fell short of true love, was well aware of the pull of her hormones, especially towards so handsome a boy. Madame Petiot had uttered warnings and then shrugged. It was the way of the world, and no great harm would come of behaving as nature intended. Jules could do very much worse.

Perhaps she was right. It is a moot point.

The two were in the barn. Their games had progressed very close to the point at which they would have behaved much as nature intended but with minor variations, when the door was dragged open. They stilled, but without any great haste. Monsieur Petiot would not have cared. But the arrival was a German soldier who had become separated from his unit. He was rather fat, half drunk and not very well shaved. He observed the scene through narrowed eyes and then gestured to Jules to leave. When the young man began to protest, the German drew his bayonet. Jules ran for it. The German stuck his bayonet into the oak boards. Helen tried to run but she was grabbed and pushed back down into the straw. She struggled but there was ample rope and twine to hand and the German was heavy and kneeling on her elbows. When she was secured the German retired to a corner of the barn and took the pee that had been his reason for entering in the first place.

Helen had been prepared to surrender her virginity, but not to have it snatched away by somebody other than the intended recipient. The act of urination did not take very long, but it was long enough for her fury to reach flashpoint. It also gave her time to loosen the binder twine round one of her wrists. While the German's interest and concentration were on removing her underwear, she freed her hand and moved with the speed of a rattrap. She snatched the bayonet out of the wall and rammed it up under his ribs with all her strength. It took enormous effort to pull it out again against the grip and the suction but she put her back into it.

When Jules returned, bringing a pitchfork and his father with a shotgun, the German was undoubtedly dead. Helen was leaning against a post, panting and wild-eyed. When she had calmed, he asked her, 'You are ... all right?'

She lifted one side of her mouth. 'I am just as I was. He did not have time.'

'That's good.' Jules bowed his head. 'But I ran away.'

'You did just as you should,' she assured him. 'If you had tried to fight him, we might both have been killed.'

Jules looked happier, but he seemed afraid to touch her after that.

Within a day, dispositions had been made. The German had been buried deep, with all his accoutrements except for his rifle and some papers, both of which vanished into the hands of the Resistance. The occupying force had no idea where the man had got to and wrote him off as a deserter. There were no repercussions.

Helen was hurriedly conveyed to a nearby château where six British airmen were already ensconced in the cellars. They had been on their way towards repatriation through Spain, but somehow it was known that D-Day was not far off, and it had been decided that they were safer where they were. She helped to minister to the airmen. But it was an active time for the Resistance. Instructions arrived daily from London by way of the very secret radio cleverly hidden in the back of a large, genuine radio which was so obviously non-functioning that the Germans, on their rare visits, ignored it. Carefully planted misinformation had led to the diversion of troops towards the south and sabotage of their movements became a priority.

Helen proved her value. Her face had a cast of innocence that was later to prove an irresistible lure for men, but which also enabled her to carry messages, arms or explosives with little risk of being stopped and searched. At first she embarked on those adventures with a queasy stomach, fear chewing on her vitals. Soon her attitude became neutral. In the end, she discovered that she was enjoying the adrenaline rush and the battle of wits.

Inevitably she became drawn into taking part. On one occasion the leader of a unit was taken shortly before the arrival of a train that was reportedly laden with looted treasures. The railway bridge was guarded. The remaining men were lost without a leader and were on the point of dispersing. When Helen took command there was no protest. The operation was initially success-ful, the guard was disposed of, permanently, and the bridge was blown. The explosion and firing attracted the attention of another

German unit and the train was recaptured, but it was never determined just how much of the treasure ever reached Berlin. It was a time when many Germans were hiding away looted treasures in the hope of making a quiet disappearance in the event of defeat.

On the whole Helen was, if anything, rather disappointed when the first Allied troops to arrive discovered that her carefully hidden passport was in fact British and arranged for her to be repatriated to Britain. Her farewell to Jules was affectionate, even passionate, but it took place on a crowded railway platform.

Two

Her grandparents in Devon extended a qualified welcome to the almost penniless granddaughter whom they had never seen. The wartime presence of a whole spectrum of friendly Allied soldiers had driven away any vestiges of xenophobia. They found that her mother had instilled in her a knowledge of the English language if anything slightly superior to their own, albeit spoken with a pleasing accent. She was even well read in English, thanks to her mother's collection of the Everyman series of the classics.

Post-war austerity was a hard time for the elderly, but she was not a burden to her grandparents. Her service with the Resistance was vouched for and counted as if it had been with the military. She quite accepted that her days of adventure were over, at least for the moment. She received a modest grant for further education and attained on top a very good scholarship to Exeter University. She set to, studying Politics and Journalism. She found the British weather cold but stimulating; the people, once one got to know them, friendly without being intrusive. The men she found less romantic than their French contemporaries and the food was undoubtedly plainer. It never occurred to her to return to France. Her acquaintance with her father's country was with the peasantry, and she had no intention of serving in their ranks. Her English relatives, though impoverished, belonged to a higher stratum of society. Once she had learned how to handle an umbrella in a breeze and had mastered certain differences of culture, mostly concerned with the dinner table, she found Britain to her liking.

Emerging into the harsh world again with her degree clutched in her hand, she found that real life was cold and hard, full of school-leavers and returned servicemen and women all competing for such jobs as a debilitated economy could provide. She considered applying for work as a translator with the United Nations but, rightly or wrongly, judged that it would lead only into a dead end. Her sights were set more on the editorship of a major national daily. But first she had to set foot on the ladder. She accepted that she would have to work for a pittance, perhaps supplementing her income by waiting at table part-time. On this hand-to-mouth basis she worked briefly for the *Dundee Courier* and the *Easthampton Gazette*.

A glance at those who have made it to the top in almost any profession will usually assure us that, however much skill and determination played their part, luck had a great deal to do with it. Helen, after narrowly failing to get several more lucrative jobs, contrived for once to be in exactly the right place at exactly the right time. She had come a distance and put up in a local hotel in order to attend yet another interview at yet another local paper in the hope of a modest improvement in status and salary.

There were several other contenders for the job and she was fairly sure that she was not in the running. After breakfast in the hotel, she took a walk out of the town along the towpath beside the upper Thames to consider her future. The prospect of majestic trees beside the shining water was pleasing, but it seemed to her that her own prospects were not encouraging.

She had reached a low point in her deliberations when she heard the squeal of skidding tyres and the sound of a car bursting through the hedge. A moment later, a large car wallowed down the slope, missed her by no more than six feet, scared a swan off its nest and plunged into the river. Another car stopped on the road above but then drove rapidly away towards the town. The swan circled twice and then settled on the water.

There was nobody in sight except for a few strollers on the far bank and the occupants of the car. These seemed to consist of a lady and a gentleman who looked somehow familiar. The car, after drifting some yards away from the bank, was settling in the water. The lady had wound open her window, which seemed to Helen to be a less than good idea, as it allowed the car to fill and settle more quickly. The lady was panicking. She forced herself out of the window and clambered on to the roof, screaming all the while. The man remained seated. The car sank lower. It seemed to have touched down on the silty bottom and to be settling into it.

Somebody had to do something and there was nobody else around. Helen dropped her bag and took to the water, shuddering slightly at the unfamiliar sense of wet clothing. She had always been a strong swimmer. The swan, resenting this intrusion into its territory, approached, hissing. Helen chose the rudest expression that she could think of to tell it to go away. The wording was in French but the swan seemed to get the message. The lady squatting, frog-like, on the roof of the car, appeared to be expecting immediate rescue, but she was safe enough where she was, whereas the man was running out of time. He seemed to have taken a knock on the head. The pressure of the flowing water made it difficult to open the door, but with a great effort Helen managed it. Something else prevented her from hauling out the man. She took a deep breath and sank down, groping for his feet. They were jammed among the pedals. She had to make a choice between doing further damage or letting him drown.

Just when she needed help, help arrived in the form of a young man swimming strongly beside her. He seemed to be about to attempt a gallant rescue of the lady on the roof, but Helen was adamant. 'Hold his head up,' she gasped.

The young man caught on immediately and supported the other's head, keeping his face out of the water. Helen dived again, pulled and jerked and somehow dragged the man's feet clear of the pedals. She rolled him on to his back to float him to safety. The young man took the lady in tow and the small convoy headed for the bank, escorted by the swan.

As she neared landfall, she became aware that they now had an audience. She learned later that the car that had driven off had held a man who, a non-swimmer himself, had sensibly rushed to call for help, but had then hurried to the local paper, the very paper that was considering her worthiness for a job, to warn of a drama in progress. The photographer who had accompanied the reporter to the scene was an enthusiast as well as a professional, and he had brought his cine camera. The ambulance had attracted the attention of several people who had nothing better to do and so it went on. Thus as the protesting lady and the semi-conscious man were hauled up the bank there was a small round of applause.

Helen and her helper were unhurt, although she now realized that her skirt, which had been hampering her movements, had become almost entirely lost. (Most of it was found later, caught on a door hinge of the sunken car.) They disdained any help from the ambulance personnel. The media people were more persistent, but Helen's new friend was unusually firm. First gallantly removing his shirt to tie around her waist, 'We're both soaking wet, cold and part-drowned,' he said. 'Either let us get dried and comfortable or bugger off,' he said. 'Pardon my French,' he added to Helen. 'My name's Allan Drysdale. I have a flat just across the road. I can offer you a hot bath, towels and nourishing soup. After that, you could try on some of my clothes or wait for my clothes horse to do its best with what remains.'

'I'm Helen Mercier,' she said. They shook hands. 'And that wasn't French,' she said. 'The French would have said *va t'en.*' In case any of the growing audience understood French, she did not repeat what she had said to the swan.

He laughed. Still laughing, he recovered her bag for her, then led her up the embankment and across the road. A straggle of large houses extended, ribbon development style, from the fringe of the town, and one of these had been divided into flats. His flat was on the first floor. The media would have followed them indoors but the man (who if he didn't play rugby should certainly have done so) prevented their entry, and they were left fretting in the narrow front garden while the couple took turns in the quite opulent bathroom. Her sodden clothes were rinsed and hung up to dry. She was soon dressed in a shirt and trousers with the sleeves and cuffs rolled up and the waist belted in. Rather than present a more comical appearance than was absolutely necessary, she took care with her make-up and hair, brushing her hair out as she dried it in front of his oven while enjoying the promised soup.

All this had taken time. They were amazed to see how the crowd from the media had grown. They only learned later that the story had quickly achieved newsworthiness fit to rank with the Second Coming or even a film star's baby. A story, of course, becomes twice as valuable if there are pictures. The availability of both still and moving images featuring two ladies whose clothes had suffered damage or loss, along with a swan that had decided to make the best of the disturbance by being included in the pictures, saved the story from being relegated to the radio and had caused a reporter to follow up the unfortunate couple to hospital. There it emerged that the man was a rich and very senior duke. His name was well known although his face was not. The lady was a duchess. Unfortunately, she was not his duchess.

All this was unknown to Helen when they emerged to face the media from the front steps. She was relaxed in front of the cameras – nobody had told her that she should be nervous – and she spoke easily, making a funny story of it when she could introduce a little humour rather than appear to be boasting. She had been in Britain long enough to know better than to appear boastful. The interview was almost finished when a minor reporter asked her, 'Had you ever seen either of them before?'

In all innocence, she replied, 'Yes. I saw them come downstairs together while I was having breakfast in my hotel this morning.'

The resulting scandal rumbled on for years. Meanwhile, Helen's appearance on the newsreels and on television was deemed photogenic. She received the offer of a job from the local paper at an improved salary, but a much better offer of a job as a television reporter. She jumped at it, guessing that that way lay the future.

TV at that time was in its infancy. She had to be prepared to do anything. At first she was sent out to cover criminal trials and the doings of the royal family. Between times she might be required to read the news or the weather forecast or to interview a minor celebrity. Somehow she found time to marry Allan Drysdale, but by then she was working under her maiden name. Helen Mercier somehow sounded more international and sophisticated than Helen Drysdale and accorded well with her accent, so she retained it for work.

She was an instant success, launched on what was to become a long and successful career. The combination of good looks with accurate reporting and a command of English that did not include 'basically' or 'in terms of' made her almost unique in the world of broadcasting. She never resorted to the lazy evasion of 'coming to terms with' but always struggled to find the exact definition of the subject's reaction; and when, rarely, she used the word 'anticipate' she did not mean 'expect'. By the time that her son

James was born she was sufficiently well established to take time off for the purpose without letting her career lose momentum, and soon she was earning enough to provide him with a nanny and the best in education. When possible, she took him with her on her trips to sporting events or film festivals, but when his attendance was impossible she would explain very carefully why this was so, and he accepted her good intentions as being for the best.

She found that she was making this apology more and more often. War reporting took a heavy toll of journalists, but she was a survivor and there was a growing demand for her services in the trouble spots of the world. When the BBC lost its monopoly in broadcasting she transferred her allegiance to the independent networks, and this allowed her to repeat her commentaries in French. This repeat income was much appreciated by her cameramen – for short periods at a time – but ulcers and nervous breakdowns necessitated their frequent replacement, and as technology improved she often acted as her own photographer.

Just after the Bay of Pigs, she landed in Cuba from a small boat and obtained an interview with Fidel Castro. She shared a foxhole with Kate Adie. She became almost a familiar figure in Northern Ireland, where the impartiality of her reporting gained her a degree of respect, although she twice survived assassination attempts. She was seen on television, naked but face down, with a delighted army surgeon picking fragments of shrapnel out of her bottom. It was said that she would sleep with anyone, regardless of race, religion, colour or even gender for the sake of a good story, but this was untrue. She prided herself on limiting her favours to people whom she liked and respected.

But even a lady with a heart-stopping smile and a talent for the erotic arts may lose her power to attract with time. A parachute jump over the Falklands convinced her that her days of physical adventuring would soon be over. She had money put by. In preparation for the inevitable retirement, she bought a small house in a Sussex village. It was larger than it appeared, and though it was not thatched, it looked as though it had been meant to be so. Her own chat show postponed retirement for a few years, but her heart was never in it and she had lost whatever taste she might have had for interviewing minor and talentless celebrities. Eventually she settled to a life of leisure, playing gentle tennis, tending her garden and walking her dogs. If some event occurred that the moguls deemed suited to her special talents of reportage, or if an interview was required with one of the great and possibly good with whom she still had a friendly working relationship, she would emerge from retirement, do a noteworthy job and retire again.

She had found peace.

Three

Helen's son, James Drysdale, appeared to be a less dynamic personality than his mother. He seemed rather to have inherited the aesthetic abilities of his father and some of the patience of the French peasant quarter of his ancestry. Allan Drysdale had tired of being left to his own devices while his wife enjoyed the travelling and the kudos and earned most of the money. He had transferred his affection to the publishing assistant who usually commissioned him and who would at least be around while he pursued his calling as a book illustrator. There was a mostly amicable divorce and James's time thereafter was divided between his parents.

He grew up wise in the ways of the world

and *au fait* with current affairs. From his father he got his skill with line and colour and from his mother an understanding of the worlds of television and show business. He had plenty of skill, almost brilliance, as a set designer, but even if he had been totally without talent, few producers would have resisted his mother when she went on the attack. He was seldom without work.

If Helen had not been *en route* from Zimbabwe (where Independence had been declared) to Vietnam at the time, she might have warned him not to marry the starlet who caught his eye. His mother, out of her experience, would have seen that the girl did not have a capacity for constancy. Marriages in Helen's dynasty did not tend to endure. That marriage lasted two years. The first indication that James had that all was not well was when his wife, who did care for him in her fashion, began teaching him to cook. In the ensuing divorce the starlet, who never did progress much further up the ladder, gave up all right to her baby boy, to the annoyance of her husband, who had no great desire to be saddled with an infant just

33

as his career was getting off the ground.

As soon as Helen was back in Britain and the cuts where shrapnel splinters had been removed from her back and bottom were healing nicely, James presented her grandson to her with a conspicuous show of generosity.

'And what am I supposed to do with this?' she enquired.

'If you can't manage...'

Those words were more potent than a red rag to a bull. Bulls are almost colour-blind. Helen had never admitted that anything was beyond her.

James then vanished across the Atlantic to the USA, where he shuttled to and fro between Hollywood and New York with occasional side trips to Canada, grabbing for himself the cream of the commissions to design sets for the film, TV and theatre trades. Whenever he remembered, he sent cheques.

Helen opened up her Sussex house, which had largely lain empty during her most recent absences. By paying over the odds, she managed to engage a gem of a nanny-cum-tutor and disappeared abroad again. But the frailty of age was overtaking her and soon she was spending more and more time at Bracken House with David. When he was mature enough for boarding school, they said farewell to the nanny-tutor. Thereafter, Helen restricted her assignments to the school terms or allowed David to stay with a school friend. He was a likeable boy and handy with tools, so he was usually welcome.

David broke the pattern. As a family, intelligence was not in short supply, but it usually surfaced in the form of an aptitude for one or other of the arts. Instead, he had an innate feel for machinery. Despite a particular rapport with vehicles, he showed no desire to emulate his grandmother by wandering the globe. After gaining a degree in mechanical engineering he settled down locally, lecturing part-time at both the local technical college and the university.

At first he lived at Bracken House with his grandmother. The two were friends rather than relatives, but space soon became inadequate. Besides, he was human. There were occasional girls and although Helen understood the physical needs, perhaps rather better than he did, she was becoming a respected figure locally. With Helen's help he purchased the renovated Gabriel Cottage, complete with an adjacent barn, within a mile of Bracken House. Here he had space to install the machinery that he craved. He watched the papers for announcements of sales at defunct garages and engineering workshops.

He began slowly, but the death of his father in a freeway pileup in Los Angeles suddenly gave him a degree of independence. This did not go to his head. He continued lecturing, repaid his grandmother what she had advanced him and replaced some of his equipment with more sophisticated versions with computer controls.

One of the sales that he attended produced a totally clapped-out E-type Jaguar. It had been raced, damaged and then left standing out of doors. He bought it at once for a song, and set about a total rebuild to a very high standard. The bodywork and mechanical parts were well within his abilities, but for upholstery, carpets and trim he did not take any risk of spoiling the ship for a ha'p'orth of tar. When Helen saw one of the accounts she said, 'Have you gone off your chump?'

It was a reasonable question. David, who had been rolling along under his own momentum, considered it carefully. Then he fetched one of the motoring magazines and showed her the going prices for mint-condition examples of one of the world's iconic designs. 'There seems to be a smidgeon of method in your madness,' she admitted. Anyway, it kept him out of mischief, most of the time.

During the process of renovation, work was often interrupted by visits from enthusiasts, some in need of help and advice, others wanting to discuss and admire. A columnist from the premier motoring magazine for enthusiasts came by appointment with a photographer; he stayed for most of a working day and probed into the stratagems necessary in restoring a car for which parts are no longer made. The resulting article brought a spate of interested visitors and several enquiries from other restorers of classic vehicles seeking advice.

Work was nearing completion when Henri Lemaître introduced himself. Unlike Helen, who had retained her French accent when it might otherwise have faded away, he was struggling to sound more English than the English. He was a lean man. The black of his hair was matched by his eyebrows and the tuft of beard on his chin. He impressed David by offering to lend a hand and spending several evenings meticulously applying leather to door panels and polishing walnut trim.

When the last nut was tightened, Henri wiped an imaginary smear off the shining bodywork and the two stood back. It was an early summer's day, warm without being too hot. Birds were singing and a light breeze was stirring the beech trees behind the cottage. Sunlight glowed on old brickwork and climbing plants, but the men only had eyes to admire the elegance of the perfectly streamlined shape, the sparkle of chrome and the mirror finish of the cellulose. 'So,' Henri said. 'What do you do next, old man?'

David decided to ignore the form of address. He already suspected that Henri had polished up his English with the aid of pre-war novels by Wodehouse. 'Drive around and enjoy it, I think,' he said. 'I'm not going to sell it yet, if ever.'

'But no. I do not think you will be satisfied until you are busy again, no? You are not the type.'

David backed the Jaguar into the barn and they pulled the dust sheet over the car. 'I expect you're right,' David said. 'Something will turn up.'

'Assuredly. I heard of another E-type, in no better shape than this was.'

David straightened his back. 'Where can I see it?'

Henri held up a hand. 'Do not hurry too much, old man. This is a collector. I hear that he is losing his sight and must stop driving and working. Also his money is almost gone. They say that he has also a Type Forty-four Bugatti. And there is an eight-horse Peugeot from 1902, but that has been in a fire, they tell me. If he breaks up his collection he has the money to go to

Switzerland for an operation that will save his sight. But you are known to be a restorer, he is a collector, he will have seen that article. If you show your face, it is known and the price it goes up, no?'

By this time, David was hopping from foot to foot with impatience. 'Anything else?'

'I think not.'

'How badly burned is the Peugeot?'

Henri gave a very Gallic shrug. 'I can find out. I'm told that it would rebuild.'

'While you're making enquiries, see if you can find out how much they would want for all three.'

'It will be a lot of money.'

'Find out anyway.'

'I will do that for you, old man.'

David found that his hand was shaking. Three rare motorcars at a blow would keep him happily occupied for the next five years or more, perhaps even ten. He needed a distraction or he would burst. 'I think I'll show the Jag off, just along the main road and back. Coming?'

Henri looked at his watch. 'I think not, old chap. I have a few phone calls to make, yes?'

He winked. 'I use your toilet before I go?'

'Yes, of course. Drop the latch when you've finished.'

David drew the dust sheet off again and lowered himself into the customized driving seat. The view along the bonnet was breathtaking – the curves, in his opinion, were as perfect as those of the most beautiful woman and far more enduring. The only sound from the engine came from the exhaust. The whole car had the tautness of the very new.

In David's desk, Henri found his account books and bank statements.

If Helen had not been away she would almost certainly have recognized the signs of the classic con trick, but she had been coaxed into making a temporary emergence from retirement in order to fly to Africa and record an interview with a president who was planning major constitutional changes. The president was an old friend who was refusing to be interviewed by anyone else. Suggestions were made by disappointed rivals that there had been intimacy between

41

them in the distant past, suggestions that neither of them either could or cared to deny.

It was the evening after her return. Her house, as always, had welcomed her with its cosiness, which somehow managed to stop just on the right side of good taste. The house-and-dog-sitter had been thanked and paid off. She told herself, for the twentieth time, that she was getting much too old for all this gallivanting around. As some women postpone admitting to forty, she was post-poning being twice that age. She had bathed away the last traces of African dust and, wrapped in a towelling dressing gown, was preparing to sleep away her jet lag when her attention was demanded by a combined ringing and knocking at her front door. She put down her mug of Ovaltine with a thump and went to the door, pulling the gown tightly around her. If the visitor turned out to be a salesperson, a political canvasser or a religious zealot, he or she would get an earful.

She had to stand on tiptoe to look though the peephole. David, her grandson, was on the step. He passed her so quickly on his way into the hall that his kiss on her cheek was like the brush of a passing butterfly. There were none of the expected enquiries after her health and the success of her mission. 'Gran,' he said, 'can I borrow your car?'

Helen could see that he was distressed, but even so she was not going to let him off with such a breach of good manners. 'I'm very well, thank you,' she said. 'And it was all a great success. How are you and what's wrong with the Jaguar?'

He pulled himself together with a visible effort. 'I'm OK,' he said, 'but I've been ripped off and the Jag's been stolen. I don't know how long he's been gone, but I know where he's going and I may be able to catch him.'

'Have you called the police?'

'He could be aboard the ferry before they finished asking questions and taking down the answers. Please, Gran.'

She had a hundred questions but she could see that he was twitching with nerves. Her heart softened. The keys of her Alfa

GTV Lusso were in her bag in the hall cupboard. She handed them over without a murmur. He thanked her, briefly but from the heart, and then he was gone.

She went to bed and slept like the dead. Time enough to worry about David's problems in the morning. They would probably go away if she threw money at them. That was one consolation for a life of stress and discomfort, spent providing for old age and just this sort of contingency, whatever it was. She had had many good friends and had obtained and followed some excellent financial advice.

She slept immediately and deeply. Ringing and hammering woke her, hours later but before she had intended to wake. The sound was so familiar that she expected to find David on the doorstep with the keys of her Alfa. From the top of the stairs, she called, 'Put the key through the letterbox.'

But the ringing was repeated. She pulled on her towelling gown and went down. Instead of David there was a policeman on the step. He looked a little surprised to be greeted by an old lady. 'Madam, are you the owner of a car?'

'I am,' she said. Her mouth was suddenly dry.

He looked down at his notes. 'Make and registered number?'

She quoted them.

'Does anyone else have permission to drive your car?'

'My grandson, David Drysdale. He borrowed it. It's insured for any qualified driver. Now tell me what's wrong.'

The policeman closed his book. 'I'm sorry to tell you that there's been an accident. A serious one. A young man, probably your grandson, is in the hospital. The car had to be cut apart to get him out of it, but he's expected to live. Here, are you all right?'

It had seemed for a moment that the world was going away from her. But years of self-reliance in the trouble spots of the world had tempered a nature already tough as steel. 'I'm all right,' she said firmly. There was no point opening up any other matters. She did not know enough. 'Which hospital is he in?' she asked. There would be a thousand things to do.

Four

One phone call to the hospital was enough to confirm the bare facts conveyed by the policeman – that David was badly injured but likely to survive. The voice, apparently that of the ward sister, added that he would not yet recognize a visitor but that a familiar voice might prove helpful if she were to come that evening. Further medical details would not be given over the phone. Helen closed her eyes for a full minute until the swimming sensation passed. But she had had a long training in detaching herself from disaster. Accepting that circumstances had changed, she began, mentally and physically, to reorganize her life and mind.

Another call, this time to the police, confirmed that her much-loved car was definitely a write-off. She mourned its passing but she refused to mope. It was only a well designed and expensive artefact, and it had been well insured. She phoned her bank to set the ball rolling, and then her insurance company for a claim form, before calling the nearest main agent. Hers was a familiar name and voice – she had hired cars, bought cars and had cars serviced there for twenty years or more. Her usual practice was buy a high quality trade-in or else to call for brochures, make a careful choice of model, facilities and colour, haggle over her own trade-in and wait patiently for delivery. This time, however, she found herself without transport and time pressed. David's everyday personal transport of the moment was a small motorcycle, a mode of transport that Helen was perfectly capable of riding but which she considered un-suitable for daily use by one of her years. Moreover, at her age she had no intention of travelling in discomfort or of suffering more than a reasonable minimum of noise. Age, she felt, should have its privileges.

The garage was the main agent for BMW but they could not furnish what she wanted off the shelf. They had several nearly new trade-ins that might serve her needs. She gave them a list of her requirements, ranging from automatic gearbox to air conditioning and told them to send over whatever came nearest to conforming. If she liked it she would keep it. She dropped the name of the Mercedes agent, to keep them motivated.

Moving around with the cordless phone tucked under her ear, she had managed, in the long intervals of hold-the-line-please and if-you-want-this-service-press-such-and-such alternating with I-am-putting-you-on-hold, to make and eat a quick breakfast and get washed and dressed. She had time to walk to David's home to make sure that all was secure. It was as well that she took the trouble. David's Golden Retriever puppy, known for the moment as Bigfoot, was housed in the back porch, very hungry and very anxious, although thanks to the cat flap the place was clean. The house and the barn had both been entered violently. The Jaguar was certainly absent and she could guess that the house had been entered in search of the keys. Drawers were open and David's possessions had been tossed around, but nothing else was obviously missing. The splintered woodwork was an affront in that idyllic setting. She used David's phone to call a local joiner to come and make all lockfast.

She brought Bigfoot back to Bracken House. There was already a car at the door. The agents did not want to lose a good sale or a valued customer. But first things came first. She fed the puppy and saw him reassured and settled with her own spaniels where he would have access to a fenced-in paddock.

The car was a nearly new BMW 540 with an impeccable service history and a very low mileage. It even had satellite navigation installed, which, at the time, seemed a ridiculous extravagance. She disliked the colour, but no doubt she would stop seeing it after a week or two. She wrote a cheque on the spot, phoned her insurers again, deposited the car salesman back at his office and set off for the hospital. She had never seen it before, which testified to the general health and caution of both Helen herself and her grandson. It proved to be a large complex, very modern, very streamlined, very well equipped, but lacking any concessions to beauty or humanity.

The vast building was bustling with activity. As she walked and stood in a lift and endlessly walked again, she sampled the vibrations in the air. She could well imagine the staff struggling with requirements that were eternally in conflict. Trying to save money and to spend it; fighting for time on overused scanners; planning surgery and worrying about superbugs; breaking bad news with sympathy and yet remaining detached; healing but occasionally killing in error; prolonging life and yet sometimes in mercy allowing the sufferer to slip away. Patients either healed or they did not and only now and again could the medical staff feel that they had made much difference one way or the other. She pushed aside the thought of a more penetrating documentary series than ever before, dissecting the hospital as an organic being. Habit dies hard, but she was retired, she told herself for the thousandth time.

She found David in the High Dependency Unit. He was bristling with what seemed an exceptional number of tubes and wires connected to several monitors. She had to look more than once to be sure that this really was her handsome grandson. Massive bruising was developing. There was some sort of cage over his feet. An elderly but apparently responsible doctor met her. He took her into a side room camouflaged as somebody's sitting room, selected a comfortable chair for her and almost patted her hand. She decided to let the sweet old lady image roll on for as long as it produced sympathetic attention. A few years earlier and he would almost certainly have recognized her, but her face was becoming less known and hospital doctors' hours are too long and too variable to allow for much regular watching of TV.

'You must understand that he's had a bad knock. His legs took the worst of it. The airbag saved his life, there's no doubt about that. You know about airbags?' he asked anxiously.

Helen had more than once been punched in the body and had her wrists singed by a deploying airbag, but she only nodded.

'We're waiting to see if any internal injuries show up, but so far the signs are good.'

'His head seems badly bruised,' she suggested.

The doctor nodded. 'We won't know how his brain has come through until he wakes up.' The doctor had restrained himself from saying 'if' or 'unless'. He seemed to hesitate before going on. It was always a problem to know how much to tell an elderly and infirm relative. 'Brains do a lot of bouncing around inside the skull in this sort of accident. There will be some memory loss, but how persistent and going how far back we don't know yet. He may never remember the accident or it may come back to him with time.'

'And his legs?'

'We have some work to do, when he's over the shock. One ankle is badly broken, the other seems to be sprained.'

'The person I spoke to suggested that it

would be helpful if there were a familiar voice speaking to him.'

'That's so. It's early yet, but if he hasn't come round soon, yes, one of his relatives should talk to him.'

'I'm all there is,' she said sadly.

'You, then. It's surprising how much gets through. Afterwards, they sometimes re-member more about what was said to them while they were asleep—' he avoided using the word 'coma' '—than they do about the accident. You can come in at any time and sit and talk to him.'

'I'll come back in an hour or two.'

She was becoming more familiar with the differences in control and feel of the new car, but did not feel ready to hurry. It took her some time to discover where the wreck of her other car lay, then to find her way to the place and finally to persuade a mechanic to prise the remains apart sufficiently for her to recover the few undamaged items of personal property that she wished to retrieve. She turned her face away from the blood that puddled on the floor-pan, shuddering instead at the state of her faithful old companion.

While she was in the city, it seemed a good time to have a meal and to shop for supplies to sustain her during her vigil. She found a small restaurant and made a careful choice from the menu.

At the next table a heavily pregnant young woman was lunching with a man, who, it was clear from the conversation, was her husband. Both, from their accents, were Irish. As they neared the end of the meal the expectant mother made a gesture that knocked over her water glass. The tumbler cracked. 'Oh!' she exclaimed loudly, 'me water's broke.' There was immediate panic, the waiters intent on getting her out before the birth became too far advanced. Seeing that the head waiter was prepared to forget about their bill in order to expedite their departure, the husband did nothing to clear up the misunderstanding.

It was nearly four hours rather than two before she returned to the hospital. She had had time to scan the new car's instruction manual while she ate. She removed the detachable front from the radio/CD player and carried it into the hospital in her bag of provisions. She had had cars broken into before, and the nuisance value far outweighed the cash value of the goods stolen. A young man with jeans and a nervous tic came out of the bushes and peered through the smoked glass. He saw the winking red light and he cursed softly. Little old ladies were not usually so clued up.

She gave details of David's medical insurance (which she had insisted on and paid for). Then she settled beside him. He was alone in a cubicle in the almost empty unit. The nurse assigned to him was delighted to be relieved so that she could visit the toilet and the canteen, and briefed her carefully on what to watch for. At first, Helen found that it felt unreal to conjure up subjects for a listener who was so obviously not listening, but her experience as a broadcaster came to her aid. She had spent thousands of hours speaking without any sign of a listener, and she told herself that this was no different. She began by telling him the story of the Irish couple in the restaurant and she thought that a faint smile passed across his face. Then she began chatting about current affairs and in particular any news of the day that he might otherwise miss. Next, it occurred to her that he might be more drawn back towards consciousness by subjects within his own knowledge. She switched into a do-you-remember? mode.

Not for the first time, she regretted having been abroad through so much of his childhood and teens, but she had made the most of what time she managed to spend with him and when she began his story, almost from the moment of his birth, more and more little incidents came tumbling forth. What spilled out was coloured by love and shaped by her years of reportage. Once or twice, when she touched on childish follies, and again when she had poked fun at a totally unsuitable girlfriend who had left him for a circus acrobat, she thought that she could again detect a smile among the bruises. She roused suddenly to the realization that the nurse, a plain girl with a square jaw and a bad complexion, was listening, absorbed. Helen was stiff. When she looked at her watch, she found that evening was well advanced. She took a snack out of her carrier bag, refreshed herself from the glass bottle of a soft drink, and resumed. The gradual reiteration of his life and times made him more real to her than the damaged and shrouded shape in the bed.

When her voice was on the point of giving out, she packed up the remains of her meal and told the nurse that she would be back.

She returned next day with an assortment of the books that he had enjoyed having read to him when he was young. It seemed a logical way to try to call him back, beginning from the earliest. She was practised at reading aloud and her slight accent added charm to an already beautiful voice. Somebody must have listened and approved. Twice a group of children from the paediatrics ward was brought through to listen to *Winnie-the-Pooh* or the *Just So Stories*. She was rewarded by the sound of their laughter and she thought that it was echoed by another faint softening of his expression among the bruises. From time to time it seemed that David might be rousing and the nurse – a different and much prettier one – agreed that the traces bore this out. But it was not until the third morning that she became aware of an added pair of eyes on her and she looked up. David's eyes were open and fixed on her.

'Gran?' he said.

'Yes.' Helen's heart was singing with joy. It was only as her body began to relax that she realized how tense she had been, but she was outwardly impassive, blinking and sniffing away the first signs of tears. The nurse – the plain one again – thought her a cold fish. David's eyes closed again. Helen went back to her reading, but found it difficult at first to keep her voice steady. David only roused once more, to say that his head hurt.

Later, the same doctor spoke to Helen. 'Don't come back tomorrow,' he said. 'His improvement's down to you, but we had him pencilled in for surgery as soon as he was over the first shock.'

'I'll see you the day after tomorrow,' she said. 'If I phone tomorrow, will I be given news of the outcome or do I have to come

58

in here and raise hell?'

The doctor laughed. He had come to realize that Helen was a much tougher and more resilient person that she usually allowed the world to see. The nurses had told him something of her background. 'I'll leave word that you're to be kept informed,' he said.

Back at the car, she put her head forward and allowed herself the luxury of a few tears.

At home, the answerphone held a message. The police wanted to speak with her. She called back and arranged an appointment for the following morning. The traffic policeman who arrived was a fatherly figure and he got the full benefit of the sweet, helpless little old lady act.

'We don't have the full picture yet,' he said. 'Maybe we never will. The doctors say that your grandson may never recover that part of his memory. So we have to consult witnesses.' He stopped, showing some signs of embarrassment.

If he was fishing for evidence that David

had been speeding or had taken a drink, the little old lady image became inappropriate. It was time to disabuse him. 'And if my grandson does recover his memory but doesn't want to admit remembering anything, you wouldn't be able to prove it, one way or the other,' Helen suggested gently. She had had some experience of head injuries and of injured persons to whom a loss of memory could be a great boon.

'That's as may be,' the constable said, giving her a reproachful look. The public was not supposed to pre-empt such thinking. 'You said that your grandson had permission to take the car?'

'I did. And he had. And it was insured for him.'

'Was he in any hurry, do you know?'

It was too early to open up the theft of the Jaguar and whatever other wrongs David might have suffered. It might be time enough when she was sure that David was relatively blameless. 'Not that I know of,' she said.

'It was a very powerful car for a lady to own,' the constable said in tones implying reproach. She thought that he had only just managed to omit the word *old*.

It had been Helen's habit always to own cars capable of sustained fast cruising. This had more than once enabled her to be first on the scene of some major event. 'I wasn't driving it at the time of the accident,' she pointed out.

'Even so...'

A lifetime in the media had taught her the knack of creative reporting. 'My grandson chose it for me. He often drives me around.'

The constable nodded. That made it all quite understandable. 'Do you know how he spent the hours preceding the borrowing of your car?'

'He wasn't with me. I only saw him for a few seconds when he collected the key. He seemed perfectly sober, but I expect you've collected a blood sample.'

The constable put away his pocketbook and accepted a cup of tea.

Later that day, she phoned the hospital. A different ward sister was reluctant to disgorge any information over the phone, but the same doctor came on the line.

'Your grandson came through surgery well and the orthopaedic surgeon was very pleased with the way it went. He should be walking again, given time. The anaesthetic has worn off but he's sleeping naturally now. While he was awake, he asked where you were. That suggests that he has all his marbles.'

'Can I see him?'

'Better not, today. Come in tomorrow, any time after ten. If he surfaces again before then, the nurses will tell him that you phoned and that you're coming back. Now you get some rest.'

'Patronizing bugger,' she said, but only after hanging up the phone.

His was good advice but easier said than done. Her earlier knack of falling asleep while all hell broke loose around her failed to come to her aid. After an hour of futile glaring at the ceiling, she had to relearn the trick of relaxing her body, muscle by muscle, and even then she had to repeat over and over, as a silent mantra, 'The surgeon was pleased with him.'

Five

Helen was at the hospital next day before ward rounds were quite finished. She was becoming a familiar face to the staff, and although her efforts had been made on David's behalf, the paediatric nurses had been grateful for a reader who could keep the more active children subdued, so nobody objected to her presence. David had been moved from the High Dependency Unit into a private room on the orthopaedic ward, which she took to be a confirmation that there was no serious organic damage. The surgeon and his entourage had just left David's bedside and the one doctor known to her looked over his shoulder and gave her a quick thumbs-up as he followed his leader into what, as far as she was concerned, might as well have been limbo. The small gesture went far towards comforting the gnawing anxiety that had followed her around like a blue-black cloud ever since the accident.

David looked tired and haggard. He was awake and capable of a smile of sorts, although she judged that it would be some days before he would be able to sit up and enjoy the view over a roofscape to the gentle hills beyond. 'Gran!' he exclaimed. 'Was I imagining it or were you here reading and talking to me?'

She stooped and kissed his forehead, carefully. 'I was here. How much do you remember?'

'Nothing much after borrowing your car. I have to accept what the police tell me. Is anybody feeding my puppy?'

She could laugh at him now. 'Don't be a knucklehead. I wouldn't leave Bigfoot to starve. He's with my lot and kidding himself that he's going to be pack leader.' She pulled up the visitor's chair and set down the carrier bag, which had become increasingly heavy with the front of her car's radio/CD player, her snacks and reading matter for herself if David proved sleepy or for him and the children if he was in the mood for more reading. She glanced at the monitors attached to him and at the bags feeding the catheter in his arm. During her career she had had some acquaintance with medical matters, what with injuries to herself and her team and interviewing the sick and injured as well as surgeons who had stunned the world with spectacularly new procedures. All looked routine.

'How are you?' She thought how trite the words were and how casually they were usually uttered. This time she waited for the answer while sending messages to God that, in the unlikely event of his existing at all, he should send her a favourable reply.

'They tell me that I'm comfortable,' David said. 'Of course, I have this on-demand painkiller plugged into me, which makes it difficult to tell, but I'm trying to use it as little as possible. I don't want to go home hooked on morphine. They seem very pleased with me. I've a slight headache still and my legs hurt, but otherwise I'm pretty good. Hungry, but good.'

'Hunger's an excellent sign. I'll think about smuggling in a few tasty morsels for you when you're strong enough. How long do they expect to keep you in here?'

'They said a very few weeks if I make good progress and if there's somebody to look after me at home.'

'There will be somebody.'

'Not just you. I don't want you working yourself into a decline over me.'

'I wouldn't attempt it,' she said. 'I remember what a rotten patient you make. When you had chicken pox you wouldn't even try to get to sleep unless you were holding your cuddly shark and I was sitting beside you nursing Teddy. I'll find somebody who can put up with you.'

He chuckled and then groaned. 'My ribs are still bruised,' he said. 'Anyway, give me credit for having grown up a little since then.'

'I would hope so. I gather that you've had the police at you already? What did they say?'

'It was only one traffic cop. I could do with more than a few tasty morsels. Something more along the lines of a steak pie would meet the case. Gran, I'm sorry about your car.'

'It was comprehensively insured. I've replaced it already. You can make good my no claims bonus when your ship comes in. What did the traffic officer say?'

'Apparently there was a host of witnesses, because the other chap had just pulled out to overtake a bus and went head-on into me. He's in here and in a worse state that I'm in, poor sod. General opinion seems to be that he didn't see me because I was following an artic and it was in the way. The bobby asked me what speed I thought I was doing and I said that I couldn't remember a damn thing. I don't suppose that I was exactly dawdling, but when the bobby realized that I wasn't going to break down and confess to anything he admitted that, according to all those witnesses, I was following that artic at the time. I may have been over the limit a few seconds earlier and no doubt I'd have been over the ton as soon as I could get past, but as it happens I'm in the clear.'

Helen relaxed. With the threat of a dangerous driving charge lifted, other problems
could be tackled one by one. 'Well, that's
one piece of good news,' she said. 'A prose-
cution for speeding would have been the last
straw. Perhaps I should get a Reliant Robin
to use as a spare car and for you to borrow
from time to time. Now tell me more about
what led up to all the fuss and flapdoodle.'

'If I'd been in the same place at the same
time in a Reliant Robin, he'd have killed me
for sure. Let me think for a moment.' He fell
silent and closed his eyes. A change in his
breathing told her that he was asleep. It was
all part of the recovery process, so she took
out her book and read patiently for twenty
minutes until he roused.

'I'm back with you.' His voice was strong-
er and even held a trace of amusement.
'Where were we?'

'You were about to spill the beans.'

'So I was. You want to know what that
bastard did to me?'

'I do,' she said, 'but start from the beginning.'

'Right. He turned up just after that article

68

about the Jag and me.'

'Name?'

'Oh yes. Henri Lemaître, or so he said. He turned up and introduced himself as a lover of fine cars, which is a very French thing to be. He was quite knowledgeable and it wasn't the kind of knowledge that could have been swotted up just to take me in. He was willing to turn up and give me a little help. He was good with his hands, which, I suppose, biased me in his favour. Also, he knew his way around the vintage car dealer-ships and he found me several bits and pieces in better shape than the ones I'd managed to collect.

'Then, just as the E-type was virtually finished, he said that he knew of another one in tatty condition. Like a mug I showed interest, so then he mentioned a couple of other cars, a 1902 Peugeot and a Bugatti, all three belonging to a collector who was losing his sight and needed money for an operation. He came up with photographs and reports.'

'He would, of course,' Helen said. 'Did you see these cars for yourself?'

'Well, no. He pointed out that I'm a known restorer and that the price would go up if I showed my face.'

'And who would be going after antique and decrepit cars except a restorer? The photographs were probably taken in the workshop behind the National Motor Museum. Reports would be easy to fake. Didn't it occur to you that it had all the makings of the classic con?' She checked herself quickly. His confidence would be shaken enough without her adding to his woes. 'Never mind, go on.'

'I suppose I was ready to believe because I wanted it to be true. I mean, those would be mouth-watering cars, a restorer's dream. He promised to find out more. And like an idiot I went off in the E-type, leaving him to lock up the house for me and making it easy for him to scout out just how much I was good for. You see, he was a friend.'

'I do understand,' Helen said. In her experience, when a man gave another man his friendship he gave him also his unconditional trust. Women were usually more sensible ... or less trusting. 'Go on.'

'And he came back a couple of days later with more photographs and a glowing description. He suggested a price that was just within my means if I stretched it a bit. I must have been the ultimate sucker, the con artist's dream.'

His grandmother sighed. 'Better men than you have been caught out by worse stings,' she said. 'Let's skip over what must have been a horrid shock for you, and talk about the moment when you realized that you'd been had. When you arrived on my doorstep, you said that you knew where he'd be heading. How was that?'

David was silent. She thought that he might have dozed off again but it turned out that he was only struggling to make order out of a chaotic period at the very threshold of his memory. 'I knew that he was staying at the White Bull in the village. I was supposed to catch a train and go to speak to a vintage car club in the West Country, so I took the motorbike to the station. I was about to buy a ticket when my mobile phone went off. The caller said that somebody had cocked up the bookings and the lecture room wasn't available, so could we put it off for another occasion. I got on the bike again and trundled home and that's when I found that the barn was standing open and the E-type had gone. I suppose he'd chosen that day because he thought that I wouldn't even know that I'd been ripped off until that night. It only took two phone calls to establish that there were no cars. The money was already out of my bank.

'I dashed down to the White Bull. He'd gone, of course, but he wasn't expecting me to turn up again just yet so he may not have been hurrying. And it happens that I have a useful contact at the White Bull.'

Something in his voice aroused Helen's suspicions. 'Oh yes?'

'Yes. Trust you to guess. A girl, of course. She'd heard him on the phone, making a booking for a car to go over on the ferry that night. And she remembered something else. A letter had come for him with a French stamp on it. It was postmarked Liverac, in the Dordogne. It stuck in her mind, she said, because Cyril, the landlord, has a liver and white spaniel. Silly, really.'

72

'But helpful. Don't bother to tell me the rest,' Helen said. Her spirit was rising. Liverac was close to what she still sometimes considered to be her home country. Perhaps it was a sign. 'If you'd waited to call the police, he'd have been out of the country before they'd finished asking you to spell every name, and your little motorbike wouldn't have caught up with the Reliant Robin that I mentioned. So you borrowed Granny's car. Were you going to run him off the road ... with Granny's car?'

He gave a quick smile from among the fading bruises. She was pleased to see that his teeth were still complete. 'My thinking hadn't got that far ahead. I was vaguely hoping to stay on his tail until he stopped and then to call the nearest cop, but that's just about where my memory cuts off.' He closed his eyes and turned his face away. 'I'm sorry, Gran. I've made a proper balls of it, haven't I?'

'You could put it like that. Your barmaid didn't happen to spot a return address?'

'She isn't a barmaid, she's a trainee manager.'

'Same difference. No need to get sensitive about it. I haven't lived all these years without realizing that a young man has some needs. I'm only happy that you're taking it straight. Just don't leave me any great-grandchildren to worry about. Well?'

'Well what? Oh, no, if there was a return address she didn't remember it. So, do we tell the police all about it?'

'Let me think,' Helen said. 'After losing so much time, it's also lost some of its urgency. The registration plates may have been changed, were probably changed before he even reached the ferry. If a letter reached him, the name you knew him by – Henri Lemaître, was it? – might be real; on the other hand, it could have been from somebody in the know. Do you know where there's a photograph of him?'

'No, I—' He stopped. 'Yes, by God, I do. There's one in my camera, maybe two. I was taking shots of the Jag in its finished state and he found himself in the background. He didn't seem too pleased. I suppose that should have told me something.'

'So unless he was daft he's pinched your

camera. We're talking about the digital one? The *expensive* one?'

David opened his eyes again and he managed another smile. 'Yes. But he can't have pinched it because I had it with me when I went to the train. I left it at home when I came to borrow your car.'

'So unless he'd already taken the memory card out of it, we have one or more photographs.' She thought. David waited patiently. 'I think I might just pop over and take a look around,' she said at last. 'Can you exist without my visits for a bit? Or will your trainee manageress come in and hold your hand?'

He laughed for the first time. 'Not a hope,' he said. 'When I sought her out to ask about Henri, she was setting her cap at a visiting company director. I think she'd only been buttering me up in the hope of having her photograph taken with the Jaguar. I can assure you that there are no other girls for the moment although one of the nurses has been giving me my bed-baths in a rather suggestive manner. I can survive if you send me in a few books from the second shelf in my study. The ones I haven't read are at the left hand end.'

'All right, my dear boy. Don't worry if you don't see me for a while. I'll keep in touch by phone. But don't hope for too much. Now tell me everything you can remember about him.'

'That won't take long. But first...' There was a long pause.

'First, what?'

He sighed. 'I'm not sure whether I should tell you this. Perhaps you'd be happier and more clear-headed not knowing. But you're a tough old boot and this may give you a fuller notion of the man. What really made me furious, and the real reason that I was going after him, was because of the photograph of you, the one you gave me. Not the posed one from my sitting room, the snapshot of you in Africa that I keep hanging over the bench in the barn. He'd taken it out of the frame and drawn on it, not very politely. That made me more furious than just being ripped off. I was going to punch his lights out. I could have done it, too. He isn't a man of violence, he's more your

76

cerebral crook.'

'Good. Did he know whose picture it was?'

'I think I mentioned once that it was of my grandmother. Why?'

'I was wondering whether he'd recognize me if he ever set eyes on me. But if I'm remembering the right photograph, my face was in the shade and turned half away. I wouldn't even recognize myself in it. And now I must love you and leave you. And if I'm going to leave you, there's no point hoarding my lunch. Could you use a sandwich?'

'Could I!'

They shared her lunch and a thermos of better coffee than the hospital could provide.

Six

It took Helen most of a day to make her dispositions. She was well practised at making quick departures to almost anywhere, but that had been in days when she had always been half prepared and more than half expecting the sudden demand that she leave immediately for somewhere hot and unfriendly. This time she had David's house to secure. Choosing the right clothes, suited to a wide variety of contingencies and weathers, took longer than the packing of them. She made a further selection from among the gadgets that she had accumulated during a career that most would call reporting but which she sometimes thought of as snooping.

The services of the house-and-dog-sitter

were re-engaged. (That lady was a widow who counted on such windfalls as an essential part of her reduced income. She also enjoyed escaping from the small house that she shared with three friends in similar circumstances, but she made great play of several other but probably fictitious engagements in order to demand a bonus and compensation for the short warning.)

After consideration, Helen decided that excessive haste, which would mean flying out immediately and hiring a car on landing, would gain very little. There would be certain items in her luggage that she would not wish to expose to airport scrutiny. In the past, she had usually been provided with a driver. If she had to relearn French traffic laws and acclimatize to road signs appearing in unexpected places while she negotiated a backhanded multiple roundabout, she would rather do it in her own car which, new to her as it might be, had all the controls roughly where she expected them and was becoming familiar enough to be driven without more than occasionally conscious thought. Also, her luggage would be limited if she flew. She was a good sailor but it had always taken her two days to become used to the motion of a ship. She told her travel agent to get her a booking for herself and her car by way of the Channel Tunnel. The long drive might be hard on elderly joints, but at least the seats were comfortable.

One urgent task before sealing David's house was to find his camera. It evaded her for so long that she thought the Frenchman must somehow have secured it, before she came across it in the pocket of a coat in his hall cupboard. The memory card was intact. She scanned through the pictures on the camera's monitor. Among the later shots were several of the E-type Jaguar, two of them including a figure that must be that of the Frenchman. A career in reporting had kept her familiar with all forms of photography. She had a digital camera of her own but had never equipped herself for processing the photographs. David's computer and printer were always available. She connected the camera to his computer and called up the images from his memory card. The same man appeared in the two shots.

She printed and cropped them and zoomed in on the face in the better image. In the first, the man was leaning over the E-type with a polishing cloth in his hand. His face was turned half away but the line of his cheek and jaw would be unmistakable. In the second shot, taken later, he had begun to straighten up and his hand was half raised as if to put the cloth between his face and the camera. They lost a little definition in enlargement. She tried again using the high-definition facility.

The results this time were sharper. The man looked carefully groomed despite his efforts on the car; she decided that he was dapper. His thin face featured high cheek-bones, a slightly distorted nose and a mouth that could easily be imagined with a bitter twist to it. She decided that she would not have trusted him, but perhaps that was hindsight? Or was it that he bore some physical resemblance to a Spaniard who, after promising undying love, had made off with several valuable traveller's cheques? The fact that the money had been in her stocking top somehow made the betrayal worse.

David had hidden away the desecrated photograph, whether from her or from himself she could only guess. She found it at last, hastily buried under dirty clothes in the bottom of his laundry basket. Either David or the Frenchman had replaced it in its frame. She was shocked by the vicious humour of the attack. The photograph had shown her standing in a pale dress against a background of sand, giving the vandal plenty of pale background on which to draw in black felt-tip, beneath the photographed head, a scene of debauchery that shocked her, worldly-wise though she was. She replaced it where she had found it. What she had most wanted to know provided the only comfort. It showed her face in the shade of a broad brim. Lemaître would not recognize her out of context and from a memory of that photograph. But the desecrated photograph had produced a secondary effect. It had raised her reaction to the crime from a desire for justice to a boiling fury. Helen wanted blood.

She had a few minutes in hand but she

needed them. She remembered to include the medication for her tiring heart. She packed her luggage into the car and set off, detouring slightly to drop off a parcel of books at the hospital.

Her tickets were waiting, as promised, at the Channel Tunnel terminal. She tolerated the unnatural, claustrophobic journey and was in France with enough time to put a lot of road behind her before picking out an auberge and settling for the night. She dined in a nearby café, where the cuisine was a reminder of long past. Her familiarity with the French language came back quickly.

Sticking to motorways and péage, the car could eat up the kilometres. She had consulted two guidebooks and they had agreed that the Hotel Marmande, which she remembered from her youth, was still well provided with stars. It was well placed, about fifteen kilometres from her old home and twenty from Liverac. When she stopped for lunch at Sainte-Maure-de-Touraine she used her mobile phone to call and confirm her earlier booking. The sun was becoming hot and she was glad of the car's air conditioning. Travelling with the windows down partly negated the cooling effect but she was refreshed by the scent of warm earth and of crops and flowers unfamiliar in England.

As she approached the Dordogne, the countryside was familiar and yet different. There was far more traffic, of course, since she had last seen it. There were more and better roads and some more modern buildings. The fields, mostly, were still small and unfenced except for electric fences where the few cattle grazed. The buildings were mostly houses of the golden local stone, vaguely neo-classical in style and with red pantiled roofs. There were fewer and smaller vineyards than she remembered but she had heard that wine-making in the Dordogne had never recovered after the phylloxera epidemic.

She had an uncomfortable sense of making a leap in the dark. On her previous work trips she had had a clear objective. An editor had told her, go there ... see this ... interview this or that person ... describe the damage ... predict the next disaster. She had been given backup and primed with all the relevant facts and theories. This time, nothing. She was an old woman revisiting the general area of her childhood without even a specific intent except justice and revenge. She had no standing, no connections, no motive except cold fury, steadily building, at the man who had robbed her grandson, caused his injury and defiled her image. She had once been good at picking her way through, round or between problems, but this was a new game with new rules. Unless she was lucky, she would be feeling her way in a hurry, blindfolded, along a route that she had never seen before. Well, she decided, she would just have to be lucky.

The Hotel Marmande stood in a garden ablaze with blossom. It was all that the guidebooks and her memory had insisted, a former château converted and modernized with a truly French determination to get the maximum value for the money. She was wrapped immediately in luxury. She had once been taken to lunch there by a relative of her father and had been amazed that such opulence could exist. A lifetime later, the building seemed smaller and the opulence less outrageous, but it was still impressive.

She was in time for a late dinner but she was tired and took only an omelette, a clafouti (a fruit dessert from the Limoges area) and a glass of Monbazillac. As she dined, she became aware of another great change. Most of the voices of the diners were British.

The under-manager on duty was a sallow young man with hollow cheeks and a once-broken nose. He glanced from her British passport to her name, listened carefully to her French accent and, when she had registered and gone into the dining room, he picked up the elaborately old-fashioned telephone.

Before settling down she thrust aside her tiredness and was careful to unpack and hang up her clothes. She was not always so concerned about mere appearance – a TV reporter in the field carried more conviction if embellished with a slight scruffiness – but on this trip it might be important. She slept well in a big, soft bed.

She was rather looking forward to pampering herself after the long drive, but she had become habituated to a proper, English breakfast. She would have enjoyed some toast and a brace of boiled eggs followed by real marmalade, but the waiters seemed to be convinced that anyone dissatisfied with a breakfast of croissants, *confiture* and very good coffee hardly deserved a place in their establishment. She did manage to obtain some marmalade, refusing to be palmed off with apricot jam.

She raised her eyes to look around, vaguely wondering what her next move should be, when her attention was caught by a well dressed man who entered the dining room. His figure and posture were clearly though indefinably French. She thought that he was probably about her own age. He was totally bald but, like her, he was upright and walked without the aid of a stick. Her attention sharpened when she saw that he was heading in her direction with the mildly nervous smile of one who is unsure of his welcome.

He pulled out the opposite chair. 'You permit, Madame?' he asked. She nodded. He spoke French with an accent that, she thought, had begun as local to the Dordogne and rural; a peasant's voice, but had been polished by rubbing against more up-market accents. 'But you do not remember me?'

His face was lined but otherwise not too marked by the passage of time. He was clean shaven. 'Since how long?' she asked.

'Long ago.'

From her childhood, then. Immediately, it came to her and she saw him again, smooth-faced, ten kilos lighter and as randy as a rabbit. She felt herself beaming. This must be the stroke of luck that she had been awaiting. 'Jules? It is you. If you had been dressed as a farmer I would have known you at once, but I have never before seen you dressed up like a lawyer, a doctor or a bank manager. I am happy to see you again, and looking so prosperous.'

A smile leaped across his face. 'Really?'

'Truly. But how do you come to be here?'

'I have a business near here. After the war,

88

the farm was too small to be worked economically. My father started the business, leasing farm machinery. The time was right for it. Together we built it up. When he died, I was the sole proprietor. This is where I entertain my most valuable clients. The under-manager in this hotel is to marry my great-niece. He is often on the desk and he recognized your name.'

'How would an assistant manager in a hotel that I visited once, more than sixty years ago, know my name?'

Jules paused and frowned. 'Those of us who were in the Resistance do not usually talk about it, but I may have mentioned your name from time to time. I have an old man's habit of reminiscing about the old days when I have a glass in my hand. The young people, they ask for stories of my youth and the wartime, so of course I tell them of Helen Mercier, of the German she killed and the train that she blew up – boom!' He chuckled. 'Marcel telephoned me.'

Helen carried out a rapid mental review of the *status quo* and decided that her identity need not be secret. David, whose conversation with other men was limited to vintage cars and sport (and quite possibly, outside her ken, women also), had been adamant that he had never mentioned his grandmother's background to Henri Lemaître.

'Did you ever marry?' she asked.

'But yes. I married Jeanette Bercole. You will remember her?'

'Yes indeed. She was in my class. How is she?'

'She died, three years ago, of cancer.' He sighed, and then brightened. 'But we had had a good life together. She was a good wife to me and gave me two sons. They run the business now and leave me the enjoyable duty of buying lunch or dinner for clients. Perhaps I get fat?'

'If you do, you carry it well.'

'I hope so. And now, how do you come to be here again, lovely as ever, back in the district of your birth?'

If the relationship, which had been passionate more than half a century earlier, was now to be one of flirtation, she could play that game. She summoned up a blush, a knack that she had perfected over the years. 'So we both wish. And you are the same handsome, silver-tongued devil?'

He smiled at her wryly and she could see the old Jules again. 'If only,' he said. 'But I can still make a lady happy.'

'By carrying her shopping for her? I'm sure.'

'Ah, you have not changed the least bit. You can still – what is it you say in English? – *take one down a peg or two.*' He looked sly. 'But some day we may yet finish what that German interrupted.'

As she recognized more and more traces of the old Jules under the changes that time and success had worked on this stranger, she remembered also how they had dallied in the big barn. A shiver, carefully hidden, ran down her body. She was tempted to make some laughing reference to flying pigs, but he was too old a friend, too attractive and, anyway, although her familiarity with the language had now returned so completely that she was even thinking in French, the idiom would not translate. Moreover, she had been about to search for a well-disposed old friend with local knowledge and contacts, and fate had delivered him into her lap. No, not lap, she corrected herself; that was an unfortunate expression. Hands. Fate had brought him to her and she must make the best use of her few resources. 'Your great-niece,' she said. 'This is Marie's granddaughter?'

'Marie never married. Her fiancé was killed by a stray shot as the Bosch retreated. Jeanne is the granddaughter of my brother Claude. Claude was killed in a plane crash in Algeria.'

'I remember Claude. And what does Jeanne do?'

'She is a masseuse. She works in this very hotel. It is how she came to meet her Marcel.'

For some minutes, Helen supported a rambling conversation as she was given news of childhood friends, mostly dead, and in return parted with some details of her own history. When Jules smiled, she could have been seventeen again. But she was only attending with half her mind, or less. The most active part of her brain was looking ahead, not back. She had already had fragmentary pieces of a plan in her mind, before she had even met the potential members of her team. At the mention of Jeanne's profession one small corner had given an almost audible click and suddenly a piece of the pattern was there; and, like most patterns, the first piece dictated its immediate neighbours. Others would no doubt follow.

She must meet and assess Jeanne soon. Unless the French middle class had changed radically since she emigrated, it was ambivalent in its morality. Lax morals were left to the aristocrats, the rich and the peasants. The middle class could be prudish but with a more than healthy respect for money, so that a masseuse might be a respectable practitioner or little better than a tart.

But first she must pave the way. The dining room was emptying. Her handbag was beneath her chair with its strap, which was reinforced by a wire, around the chairleg. In this way she could reach the contents but nobody could lift her money without passing three zip fasteners. It was a trick that she had learned during her years in the rougher places of the world. She bent and took out the envelope with the photographs of her quarry. She had prepared multiple copies. She placed one of each in front of him. 'You have seen this man?' she asked. 'He is known to me as Henri Lemaître. It may not be real, but he received mail in that name. It had been posted in Liverac.'

Jules took his time studying the prints. 'I think so,' he said at last. 'He resembles a man who came to my firm, several years ago. I did not meet him myself but I saw him when he arrived. He wished to buy some very expensive machinery on deferred payments, putting down a very small deposit. My sons were eager to do the deal but to me it did not look as it should. I insisted on guarantees that were never produced. Instead, we had an unexplained fire. The fire looked like an accident but I always suspected that it was an act of spite.'

'You were very wise not to accept his business. The man is a trickster. He swindled my grandson and stole a very valuable auto and some money. I have been fortunate, Jules. I have put money by. I could make good my grandson's loss. But that remains a last resort. It is a bad habit to let the young think that they can be careless with money and that their elders will come to their aid. Also, the money was meant for my old age, not for that of Monsieur Lemaître. So I have come to see if there is anything to be done about it.'

'You also are very wise. Are the police to know?'

'Not yet,' she said. 'Perhaps never. First I must know who he is, where he is, whether he still has the car and where he is vulnerable. If we can obtain solid proof, then perhaps. But between two legal systems, there could be many pitfalls.' She paused before going on. She had to make a physical effort to prevent her jaw clenching. 'Additionally, Jules, there was a monstrous insult, so monstrous that I can not bring myself to tell you about it. The law might punish him for the swindle and theft, but money and cars can be replaced. The law would take no account of the wounds to my grandson's feelings and mine. After that, who knows? I was hoping to search for an old friend, if such still lived, to help me.'

'*Et voilà!*' Jules patted his chest. 'You have found him. What can I do?'

'I knew that I could rely on you, dear Jules. You could provide me with a map. And ask your sons if they or anyone they know can put a true name or an address to the man in the photographs. It is very important that no word gets back to the man. While you do that ... I am stiff from my long drive. I would be glad of a massage.'

Jules's face split into a conspiratorial smile. 'I understand completely,' he said.

Seven

Marcel, the fiancé of Jules's great-niece, was on the desk again. Jeanne, he said after consulting a large diary beside the register, had no appointment for the next fifty minutes and she would, he was sure, be happy to attend to the distinguished guest and friend of her great-uncle.

In this he was correct. Jeanne responded to his call on the internal phone by appearing immediately and escorting Helen down a broad staircase to a massage parlour beside the hairdressing salon. All was hygienic and spotless and, although a decent privacy was preserved, there was nothing furtive about it.

What Jeanne might do in her spare time was her own business, but she gave Helen the reassuring impression of being innocent

97

or even virginal. She was small and looked delicate, but Helen could feel that she was very strong. The colour and wave of her fair hair seemed natural. It was cut tidily to frame a smile that seemed to be struggling to take over her piquant face. At work she was respectability personified. While she worked competently, gently and then with more firmness, to relieve the stiffness that two days of driving had induced in Helen's muscles, she chatted. She was well informed about current events outside the Dordogne and even worldwide. Next, Helen realized that Jeanne was probing with equal gentleness the veracity behind Jules's stories of the Resistance. Helen was able to confirm most of the tales, carefully revealing but not overdoing a becoming modesty regarding her own part in them. Recognition as a wartime heroine might, if it came to the ears of Henri Lemaître, distract him from identifying her as the grandmother of one of his victims.

'It was all a long time ago,' she said. Her voice was muffled against the massage table. 'I would have thought that all the stories would have been picked over and verified years ago.'

Jeanne's fingers hesitated and then resumed. 'Even now, people do not speak freely,' she said.

This struck Helen as strange. The Resistance had been the heroic highlight in an important historical sequence. 'But why not?'

'Partly I think it is shame. It was a period of subjection of which France is not proud. But there are other reasons. At first the Resistance was in the hands of the people—'

'Communists,' Helen said.

'Not at first. Because of my great-uncle, I read what has been written about those days and I have listened. The Communists became active when Russia joined the Allies. Then, after the war, there were many who claimed to have been with the Resistance who had spent the war hiding under the bed, and others who had been collaborators but who swore that they had only collaborated in order to get information for the Resistance. In the Resistance itself it was known for old scores to be paid off with a bullet. Then, when the Germans left, there was much looting. It became so that one only had to claim a connection with the Resistance to be regarded with suspicion. It has taken many years and even now there are disputes. Some awards for bravery are only now being given. Your name, however, is known.'

'It is? Truly?'

'Truly. When old people do remember those days, your name is mentioned.'

'No! This is fame indeed. But I was never a very important person.'

'That is not what my great-uncle says.'

Helen thought that Jules might not be an entirely unbiased commentator. She laughed secretly but tried not to let Jeanne feel the vibration. The massage appeared to be nearing its conclusion. 'I intend,' Helen said, 'to invite Monsieur Petiot to dine with me in the hotel tonight. I would be delighted if you and Marcel would join us. It is permitted for you to dine in the hotel?'

Jeanne smiled brilliantly. 'Madame Hélène is kind. It is permitted provided that we are with a guest in the hotel. Marcel will come off duty at six. I will tell him not to make me any appointments after five. I shall need time to do you credit.'

'Ask him also to make the necessary reservation for us.'

Helen found that her muscles and joints were moving almost with their old fluidity. She asked Jeanne how much she owed. Jeanne made a dismissive gesture, as if to say that there would be no charge to any friend of her great-uncle. Later, Helen noticed that the charge had appeared on her hotel bill and she had a quiet and private smile. *How very French!* she thought.

Jules Petiot had returned and was waiting when she reached the foyer again. He led her aside to a corner, usually reserved for the luggage of large parties, where they would not be overheard. 'The man in the photograph is indeed the man who came to ask about plant hire,' he said. 'My sons are sure that his name was not Lemaître and there is no record of where he was living. The secretary should remember – she remembers almost everything, sometimes too much. Every little mistake is filed away to be brought up on another occasion. But she is at a wedding today. We can ask her tomorrow.'

Helen nodded. 'Until then, I would like to be reminded of how the land lies, but I have forgotten my way around and the country-side looks quite different to an adult in a car from how it looked to a teenager on a bicycle. You brought me a map? Are you free to accompany me?'

With a flourish, Jules produced a Michelin road map and another to a larger scale. 'You permit that I drive you?'

'You can manage a car with an automatic gearbox and a right-hand drive?'

Tactfully, Jules refrained from laughing. 'I have a big Citroën. It is comfortable. I always drive with an automatic gearbox.'

She laughed at herself. 'Jules, I apologize,' she said. 'Sometimes I slip back into think-ing of you as the boy on your father's farm.'

He waggled his eyebrows at her. 'There is no need for apology while you are thinking of me as young and vigorous, with a full head of hair and still very much your slave...'

Helen led the way outside, rather hastily. The conversation was in danger of getting out of hand. As a youth, Jules had been rather tongue-tied, believing in deeds rather than words. It seemed that he had since acquired the knack of making pretty speeches and of producing them with every evidence of sincerity.

Jules's Citroën was indeed comfortable. Being driven, by a competent driver and not in her own car, enabled her to look around freely. The day was hot again and the countryside was bursting into all the vigour of early summer. The cereal crops which would be growing in Britain were replaced by what she recognized as sunflowers and maize. Fields were being irrigated by rotating sprays; largely provided, Jules explained indignantly, at the taxpayers' expense. The villages were interspersed with smaller clusters of houses, because the Napoleonic law of inheritance had led to a farm being divided ~~between~~ the farmer's children. Thus a hamlet would grow around the original farmhouse.

AMONG

They began with a voyage around the neighbourhood of their youth, pointing out to each other buildings and places that had once been the very fabric of their lives. But the stimulus of *déjà vu* soon faded. There had been changes, a building here, a demolition there, and a new piece of road as a link. The changes were less radical than they would have been back in Britain, but they were enough. This was new territory. Helen could not have faced the view of the barn where she had killed the German. They turned away.

A circuitous route brought them to Liverac, the town from which, if David's girlfriend were to be believed, the Frenchman's letter had been posted. But Liverac was now a substantial town, its edges trailing into semi-rural suburbs. They lunched on the broad pavement outside a restaurant, in the shade of an overhead vine, and watched the traffic passing by. There were few Jaguars. The sports cars that went past were mostly Japanese copies or kit-built. Helen longed to show the photographs around, but if this was Lemaître's

home ground, anyone recognizing his like-
ness might well be a friend of his, or at least
an acquaintance close enough to say,
'Somebody showed me a good shot of you
the other day. Have they contacted you yet?'
That would certainly set him on guard, and
a suspicious Lemaître would be impossible
to fool.

They took another and equally devious
route back to the hotel. Just as Helen was
losing heart and beginning to believe that
the girl in the White Bull had been mistaken
or that the letter had been posted by a
friend or a victim of Lemaître and that
Lemaître himself lived a long way away, they
passed a prosperous-looking house in a neat
garden, tucked between a wood and two
fields of sunflowers. On the weed-free gravel
driveway stood an E-type Jaguar. A man in
jeans and a checked shirt was administering
a loving polish.

Jules lifted his foot. 'That is the car?'

'Wrong colour. The car of my grandson is
dark blue and the man has hardly had time
to carry out a re-spray.' The Citroën was
sliding to a halt. 'Perhaps I should go and be

very English.'

'I think not, unless he too is British. But in this weather a rosbif would be wearing a T-shirt or no shirt at all. This, I think, is where I make enquiries.'

A postprandial somnolence was creeping over Helen – one of the less desirable consequences of age, in her opinion. But a dozing figure in the passenger's seat would add a veneer of credibility to a driver who had stopped the car to chat with an enthusiast. She put her head back and let herself doze for a few minutes.

She snapped awake as Jules reentered the driver's seat. 'He is the chauffeur to an English family,' he said, 'but he is also an enthusiast. With a little encouragement he would have whipped the cylinder head off to show me the valves. He has seen one other such model around, a dark blue one. So it seems that you are on the right track. But he did not know where it was based.'

During their half-day's tour, Helen had surprised Jules by taking an interest in the larger buildings that they passed. A granary, a mill, a large boys' school, each time she demanded to be told the precise function. It was shortly after passing the school and crossing a railway line that she pointed to a building that crowned a nearby hill. She looked between it and the map. 'What is that place?' she asked.

Jules chuckled. 'If there is one place your man will never be, it is there,' he said. 'That is the Convent of the Sacred Heart.'

When Jules set her down at the doors of the hotel, Helen accepted the customary pecks on both cheeks, but there was fervour in the salutations which suggested that Jules's friendship was not wholly platonic. She wondered how she would react if he pressed for a more intimate relationship. She was not beyond fond memories of romance, but would a Frenchman of peasant stock be so easily satisfied? Jules still carried with him the aura of romance that a teenage Helen had beheld in the masculine youth. The world would think them too old for renewal of the relationship but Helen knew in her heart that she was still seventeen, or any other age that she wanted to be.

Eight

Helen's room was spacious, comfortable and decorated with a luxurious good taste not always to be found in French hotels. It was as near as she could obtain to the hotel lobby – not, as the staff supposed, because she was nervous of fire, but from long habit. During her professional life, being first on the move had sometimes meant being first at the scene.

It was therefore convenient as well as private for her guests to convene in her room, where she had arranged for chilled champagne and a selection of nibbles. The younger couple had taken pains to present themselves smartly. Marcel wore a neat suit and Jeanne, putting behind her the clinical image of the masseuse, had paid a visit to the hairdresser next door and was very svelte in a flower-patterned dress in which the predominant yellow echoed the fairness of her hair.

Jeanne seemed shy at first. She must have been well accustomed to meeting hotel guests, but on what might be called her own territory. She had chatted freely during Helen's massage. Helen concluded that the combination of the luxurious room with the deference shown by the girl's great-uncle was to blame. They chatted stiltedly about the affairs of the day, but it was Jeanne herself who broke the ice by picking up the head-and-shoulders snapshot of David that Helen kept on her bedside table. His grandmother's camera had caught him at a pensive moment. He had, in fact, been puzzling over a problem to do with the valve timing of his motorbike, but to judge from the photograph he might have been composing a sonnet or a symphony. His hair was ruffled and a trace of romantic· stubble glowed in the backlighting of mild sunshine. The general impression was unmistakably masculine, with a romantic aspect suited to some film star or a poet.

'Who,' Jeanne asked, 'is the very hand-some young man? Surely you do not have so young a lover? Or is this a souvenir from your past, Madame?'

Helen laughed. She was never unwilling to talk about her grandson, but this occasion in particular was perfect for opening up the one topic that she was anxious to bring out into the light. 'That is David, my only grandson. He is in hospital just now in England. A motor accident. I shall phone later and speak to him.' She stopped and willed one of the guests to give her an excuse to elaborate.

Jeanne obliged. 'Who will be visiting him while you are over here?'

'The doctors. I am his only near relative.'

Jeanne was horrified. 'But how could you bear to come away and leave him?'

Helen shrugged. 'It was necessary. He was both robbed and swindled by a man who received a letter that had been posted in Liverac. I believe that he lives near here.'

She caught Jules's eye. He nodded and opened the conversational door wider. 'But

Madame, should it not be a matter for the police?'

'It should,' Helen agreed. 'But he stole the car that my grandson had spent two years restoring, a car that was an icon of its day. He also stole my grandson's inheritance from his father. And he drew, very rudely, on a photograph of me that my grandson treasures. Between two legal systems, with the only witness in hospital in a different country, what chance have I of proving these things? And, once proved, how would he be punished? Released on bail, perhaps, to disappear again. The car tied up in legal argument until it has rusted away. No. I wish to find where he is, then to learn his weaknesses. Then, perhaps, I shall make a plan. It may include the police, it may not.'

Marcel raised his weak chin. His eyes were bright. 'I would be proud to be included in your plans if you would admit me. But I do not see what is to be done.'

'Nor will you see until you are shown it,' Jules said firmly. 'Remember, this is Hélène Mercier. I have told you what she did to the German who ... assaulted her.'

Now that they were reminded of the story, Jeanne and Marcel looked at her with interest. Curiosity is always attached to the victim of a rape, even an attempted rape of sixty years ago. Helen was afraid that they might be moving on too quickly. She looked at her watch. 'Our table will await us soon,' she said.

'We have time to spare,' Marcel said. 'You must phone your grandson now, rather than awaken him later.'

The suggestion was sensible, although Helen suspected that Marcel had a lingering doubt and wanted her story to be confirmed. She gave in, to a murmur of agreement, picked up the room's telephone and asked for an outside line. Her guests listened intently as she keyed as far as the hospital switchboard and then argued her way through the hospital's telephone system. She had to fumble with words to switch back into English. At last the cordless extension was carried to David's bedside.

'Gran? Is that really you? Where are you?'

Helen found that she had to make a positive effort to stay with the English language. 'I'm in France, David. I've only been here a day, so I've nothing to report yet. How are you?'

'I am bored, but the doctors seem pleased with me. I don't seem to hurt as much as I did, but it's difficult to be sure about it. They're saying that I could get home in about a week if there's somebody there. I couldn't look after myself. I'll be on crutches.'

'There will be somebody there. David, you remember that I told you about my friend Jules Petiot and the adventures we had with the Resistance?' There was a hesitant silence on the line. She had never said much about her early life in France. She hurried on. 'He's with me now, helping me to get the lie of the land. He will help me to find your Monsieur Lemaître. I'll let you speak to him.' She handed Jules the phone.

David had hardly ever been in France, but his schoolboy French had benefited greatly from the presence of a grandmother who, while he was studying the language for an A-level exam, had insisted on all conversations being conducted in it. He chatted with Jules for a few minutes, about his injuries and about the car.

Jules said, 'Here is my great-niece, Jeanne,' and passed over the phone. Jeanne's expression did not change but her voice could have been that of a different woman. Her words were banal, but her tones were deeper, more breathy, infinitely sexual, speaking as only a Frenchwoman can speak. It was difficult for Helen, hearing those tones, to remember that the two had never met. After a minute or two she looked at Marcel, who stepped back and shook his head. Jeanne handed the phone to Helen.

'That's all for the moment,' said Helen. 'Sleep well and do whatever the doctors tell you. Yes, and the physiotherapists.' She disconnected, wondering whether David would sleep at all after exposure to the suggestiveness in Jeanne's tone of voice.

On her way to the dining room on Jules's arm, Helen could hear the whispered reproaches that Marcel was offering Jeanne and the laughter in her voice as she replied. The girl was unrepentant. 'If you were injured in hospital with nobody to visit you,' she said, 'and if a girl, even a girl who you have never met, spoke to you like that, would you not wish to recover quickly?'

Helen was in agreement. She would not have been surprised to learn that David was already negotiating for the hire of an air ambulance.

After such an introduction, it would have been surprising if any other topic had gripped the party, but they were inhibited by the presence around them of other diners, mostly chattering happily over their meal but prone to sudden silences. Helen did manage to fill in some details of Monsieur Lemaître's misdeeds, but the conversation always came back to the main question – how to track him down without alerting him. An experienced con artist, and Helen had known and even interviewed several of the breed, would have antennae ever alert for danger, and would certainly be warned by any word of strangers enquiring about his identity.

'When we have his true name it will be easy,' Marcel said. They were already at the dessert course without producing any worthwhile ideas.

'Except,' said his fiancée, 'that he will not have registered his telephone under the same name.'

'I think,' said Jules, 'that he will not have a landline phone at all. A cellphone would be the thing. With that, he could register it under any name and just answer it with "Hello".'

'You must make him come to you,' Jeanne said suddenly. 'Plant a story in more than one of the magazines and newspapers that you, an innocent old lady, have won a fortune on the Lotto and are looking for an investment. Include your own photograph with a lace shawl over your head, very old and frail. That would be irresistible to any greedy trickster.'

'It would probably interest a hundred of them,' Helen said, 'but I wouldn't mind that if it brought the one I want out of hiding. Well done Jeanne.'

Jeanne was becoming inspired. 'He is good looking, your trickster?' she asked.

'I thought,' Marcel said gloomily, 'that it

was Madame Hélène's grandson who interested you. But now you fancy the trickster?'

Jeanne laughed. 'Fool! I wished to know if
he was handsome because I wondered if he
looks like any type of job in particular? You
could publish a photograph and say that
your company wants to use this man as a
model in its advertising for a substantial fee.
No man would ever resist the offer of legiti-
mate money for being photographed.'

'That,' said Helen, 'is a beautiful idea.
Unfortunately, he would certainly recognize
the photograph and remember when it was
taken. But I have not yet shown you his
photographs. You may not think him
photogenic enough for such a ruse. Let's go
back to my room for a nightcap.'

They rose. 'We are obliged to you for a
truly excellent meal,' Jules said.

Back in Helen's room, she had made sure
that there would be a bottle of good brandy
and a choice of mixers, but there was still
life in the champagne and the ice in the
bucket had not quite melted. The two ladies
decided to stay with it. Helen fetched the
folder holding the two photographs of Henri

Lemaître. 'I scrolled through the shots still in David's camera,' she said. 'I think that these were the ones that David—'

She was interrupted by a squeak from Jeanne. 'But I have encountered this man,' she said. They waited in a dead silence while she knuckled her forehead, apparently in the belief that this would stimulate memory. 'He was a client of my friend Janine. We learned the profession together, Janine and I, and he went to her whenever his fibrosis became troublesome. Once, more than a year ago, Janine was unwell and she arranged for him an appointment with me. He wanted more than his fibrosis massaged,' Jeanne said primly, 'but he did not get it. Even if I had not disliked him he would not have got what he was after, but there was something about him that made me shiver. I might not have known him again except that this is just the angle from which a masseuse sees her client.'

'Did he pay by credit card?' Jules asked.

'He paid in cash at the desk.'

'Your friend Janine,' said Helen. 'Is she one who could be trusted to hold her tongue?'

Jeanne's nostrils flared. 'I think so. She admitted to me that she does not like the man, but she is not always very fussy. Her mother is ill and she needs the money, so she continues with the man as her client.'

'We have done all we can for tonight,' Helen said. 'Tomorrow I must see this Janine. Will you phone her and make an appointment – if possible at a time when you can come with me? We must impress on her the need for confidentiality. And now my children – and Jules – we must part. At my age even going to bed takes time. We will speak some more after you, Jeanne, have spoken to your friend Janine. But first, let us consider further. I begin to see the ghost of a plan. But if we manage to gain his interest, he will be suspicious. He will want my story to be vouched for. Who is an authority on the Resistance?'

'Comte Liverac at the Château,' Jules said. 'He speaks about writing a book. He has visited me more than once with questions.'

'Who is the comte now?' Helen asked.

'Gaspard.'

Luck, Helen thought, was just what she needed and it was being given to her by the bucketful. 'I remember him and I think he will remember me,' she said.

'How could he not?' Jules asked gallantly. He hung back as the younger couple thanked Helen and left. Again Helen had to turn her head to limit his kisses to her cheeks. He sighed. 'You were not always so coy,' he said.

'That, my friend, was about sixty years ago. You were not always so forward.'

'My affection has not cooled.'

'You have two sons,' Helen pointed out. 'Your ardour can not have been for me alone. And we are getting rather old for such dalliance.'

'But never too old,' Jules said.'

Alone in her bed, Helen drowsily considered. It was not given to every woman of her age to be courted. The experience was not unpleasant. She had once interviewed a psychologist who had given evidence in a sex abuse scandal. Off the air, he had pointed out to her the pity that so many of the elderly, and widows in particular, let their sensual life die rather than face the embarrassment entailed in renewing it. Creating new relationships meant admitting a friend, who had hitherto been at arm's length, into the secrets of a sagging body and sexual dysfunctions that demanded certain aids or techniques.

Helen herself was still capable and she still had her dreams. With Jules she had known most of the intimacies, stopping short only of the final culmination. Recalling some of them, she felt warmth through her body. He was an old friend. But, if the relationship progressed, would she be able to let down her defences?

No, she decided, she would not. Or would she?

Nine

One of the harsher facts of life is that the average hotel employee is up and about long before the average guest. At least, Helen assumed that Jeanne was an employee rather than an independent tenant. When she quitted her bed and began the lengthy process of preparing herself for another day, she found a note pushed under her door.

Madame Hélène, it read,
   I have telephoned my friend Janine. I told her no more than enough to arouse her interest. The only time that she and I are both free is from midday to 1.30. I am free after 11.30 and she is only thirty minutes drive away. I invited her to meet us for lunch at close

122

after twelve. There is a good small café close to her home where she works. I trust that this is okay?

Great-Uncle Jules phoned and asked me to tell you that the secretary remembers the man but cannot find his address.

Jeanne.

No doubt, Helen thought, the masseuse with the ailing mother would appreciate a free lunch; and so also would Jeanne. Well, if that was all that it took to keep her allies happy, so be it. She called Jeanne from the desk and said that she would be waiting in her car.

Promptly at eleven thirty the masseuse dropped into the passenger's seat and Helen set the car rolling down the hotel drive between oak trees that must have been planted before the Emperor Napoleon was born. She had started the engine some minutes earlier so that the air conditioning would be winning its eternal battle with the heat.

Jeanne spent half the journey in admiration of the car, its comfort and its gadgets, but there was something else on her mind. 'Madame Hélène,' she said, 'you will be returning to England soon to visit your grandson?'

'Without a doubt. If we can find the man, we shall have to set a trap and wait until he nibbles the bait. That will give me time to go and satisfy myself that David is progressing as I would wish.'

'I have never seen England,' Jeanne said. 'You permit that I come with you? I have a passport and I can pay my own fares.'

'There is no need for that. I should be glad of the company. You can get away?'

'This is a quiet time. Clients are not so stiff and sore while the sun shines. I speak a little English but David speaks better French.' She lapsed into a daydream.

Helen made a bid to recapture her attention. 'Your friend Janine. Did you mean that she works at home or at the café?'

'At her home.'

'Is there anything that I should know about Janine?'

Jeanne brought her mind back and considered. Any fact is obvious to the person who knows it, and that well-informed person usually finds it difficult to envisage the darkness enfolding the ignorant. To Jeanne, Janine was a fact. She simply was. 'She's all right,' Jeanne said at last. 'She's not very clever but she means well. She's good at the massage. What else to say? She's easily led. She likes men. Did you bring your photograph of David?'

Helen patted her bag. 'I have it.'

'Good. The story of a handsome young man being robbed and hurt will gain her sympathy. A little money will do the rest. She is a chatterbox about little things but she can be discreet about anything important. It is a pity that you do not have – turn left here – another grandson to coax her and a bigger pity that the thief is not another woman.'

Helen laughed. 'Whereas you do not like men at all? Or only your Marcel?'

Jeanne gave a quick arpeggio of laughter. 'Men have charm but I am not yet sure about Marcel. He is the best that offers for the moment. Perhaps he is the right man, or I can wait until the right man comes along.

Until then, I keep myself to myself. Marcel is impatient but I ask him if I am not worth waiting for. I keep my options open.'

'And Marcel? Does he keep his options open?'

'If he does not, I will scratch both their faces off.'

Helen glanced at Jeanne and decided that she was joking. She was laughing, but with just a hint of complacency.

Janine lived with her mother in an old house on the outskirts of Liverac. When the car arrived, she was already escorting an elderly man across the pavement to a chauffeur-driven car. She gave Jeanne a cheery wave. Helen parked outside the café. The hour was early and the café was almost empty.

Janine joined them within a few minutes. Her figure was dumpy, yet she walked as though she knew that the eyes of the men were following every ripple and sway. Her face was square without losing femininity. She kissed Jeanne's cheeks and responded to Jeanne's introduction of Helen with a brief *'Ça va?'*

'That was Monsieur Daudet,' she told Jeanne. 'He is very old and very stiff. He would be better served if a masseur came to visit him at his home, but he prefers me to give him his treatment. He asks me to visit him, but I tell him that I cannot drive and do not have a car. So today he said that he would send his chauffeur to bring me. But he lives at a distance of twenty minutes driving. I can see a patient in a little over twenty minutes. So I tell him that he would have to pay me three times. He is rich but he is careful. I think he will come round in the end.' She looked up at the waiter who was hovering over her. 'I will have the pasta. And so,' she continued without a break, 'perhaps if I am clever I can be paid for three appointments in an hour.'

She continued to prattle while Helen and Jeanne made their choices. When the waiter left, Jeanne waited for Janine to pause and stepped in quickly. 'Madame Hélène was a heroine of the Resistance,' she said, 'and now she has returned. She seeks the man who robbed her grandson. This is her grandson.' She laid David's photograph on the table. 'Madame Hélène, tell us about David.'

So Helen was free to expatiate on her favourite subject. She told them about David's patience and his talent with machinery and how he had brought the E-type Jaguar back from ruin into a sleek model in 'as new' condition. She described his sweet nature and how good he was to his grandmother. She had to take great care not to make him sound effeminate. As emotions and enthusiasms followed each other, she found that she could recall everything about him, even the expressions that flitted over his face. It came easily to her to sing his praises and before she finished she thought that David should have been there in her stead. Each girl was ready to melt. He could have had the time of his life.

Others were arriving in search of lunch. As she described the theft and the fraud, Helen had to lower her voice, which added to the air of another and less savoury world.

'But that is evil,' Janine said. Her indignation seemed to be genuine. 'Why do you tell me this?'

'I think that you know this man,' Helen said. She laid the photographs of Lemaître on the table, being careful to keep them away from the eyes of the other clientele.

'He is a patient,' Janine acknowledged. 'Is this the *vaurien*? I know him at once; I am not surprised at what you say. At times he seems rich, at other times, poor, which is not how the well established man lives. I took him for a gambler. His eyes are shifty and he looks at me as if he were pricing my lingerie.'

'You sent him to me, once,' Jeanne reminded her. 'But who is he?'

'He is Monsieur Laroque. That is all that I know and even that – I will save you asking – may not be his real name. He comes to me with his fibrosis, which he says is always worst when he has been in England. It is the cold and damp, he tells me. I do not know where he lives, he made sure of that. Once, he did not have enough money to pay me, but that was after he had had his treatment and so it was too late to turn him away. I demanded his address but he would not give it to me. I told him that I would call the police and he said that he would tell them that I had offered him sex for money.' Janine seemed remarkably unperturbed by the slur. 'So I said to bring me my fee next day or never come again. He did bring the money, but it was some days later, when he was in need of a further appointment. He apologized and made excuses Since then, I make him pay before I lay a finger on him. This happened after I sent him to you,' she added quickly to Jeanne.

'I would hope so,' Jeanne said. 'Sometimes you must have to change appointments. You have no telephone number for him?'

'I do. But it is a long one, a mobile number. Once or twice I have called him, just as you said, and once a recorded voice told me that the instrument was not in use.'

So near and yet so far, Helen thought. In the course of her work as an investigative reporter she had sometimes tried to get a name and address for a mobile number. In her experience it was possible, but not without the party being told. It was one of the advantages that the police had over the private citizen.

She dropped her hand into her bag and produced the rustle of banknotes. 'Would you be so good as to telephone me at the Hotel Marmande when next he phones you?'

Janine's eyes opened wide. 'But, Madame, he has phoned me only yesterday. He made an appointment to visit me on Monday at fourteen hundred hours.'

'In four days time?' Helen thought furiously. 'I would like Jeanne to give him his treatment. Will you phone him on his mobile number, please, and say that you must be away; taking your mother to visit a specialist, perhaps? You have phoned Jeanne and she is free at that time,' Helen glanced enquiringly at Jeanne, who nodded, 'so you made the booking. Will you do that ... for a hundred Euros?'

Janine blinked at the mention of money. 'But Madame, I should be losing a good client. Over the years he will pay me many times as much.'

'And no doubt you will immediately take on another client in his place. I offer you the hundred now and another hundred, of which fifty when you have treated him and another fifty in three months time if I can be sure that you have kept your mouth shut.'

'You may depend on Madame absolutely,' Jeanne said. 'She fought along with my great-uncle in the Resistance and he says that she is entirely to be trusted. If he were here, he would guarantee the payments. And now we go or I miss a client.'

'That is very satisfactory,' Helen said as she drove towards the hotel. 'Now we have four days to visit David. You still want to come? And can you get away tomorrow morning?'

'Yes to both questions.'

Helen speeded up. 'Then I have some telephoning to do.'

Ten

Helen's new car was left behind at Bergerac. They caught an early plane with time to spare and their connections connected satisfactorily.

Helen had been busy on the phone the previous evening. As a result, she had a list of things that David would like to have, either new or brought from his home, and a hire car was waiting at the airport. The hire firm had been unable to match all of Helen's requirements at such short notice and the car had a manual gear-change. Helen had not driven a car with a manual change for many years. The man in charge said that it was like riding a bicycle, an art that you never forgot, to which Helen retorted that she had never ridden a bicycle

133

for sixty years.

Helen was rarely at a loss. It was her habit to take up any challenge. She believed that any task that was within her strength was also within the bounds of her dexterity. She was quite accustomed to more or less simultaneous use of the accelerator, foot brake and steering wheel, plus any minor controls that might be called for at the time. She decided that she could well add the co-ordinated use of clutch and gear lever. Grasping all of her courage and uncomfortably aware of Jeanne's white knuckles in her peripheral vision, she set off; but halfway along the service road, when she tried to change up, she found that coordination between her foot and her hand had lapsed. Her mind went blank, the gearbox screamed at her and the car coasted to a halt. Passing traffic hooted at them.

'Do you drive?' she asked.

'But yes. I have a Deux Chevaux.'

'Very well. You drive.'

They exchanged seats. When Helen opened her door, passing traffic became frantic. Jeanne refused to step into the road. She climbed over the gear lever, attracting whistles from a road gang. She set the car moving. Soon the car's engine was again protesting. She trod on the brake in mistake for the clutch and the car tried to stand on its nose. They set off again. Jeanne de-clutched successfully but groped in vain for the gear lever. Helen changed up for her. 'Keep *left*,' she yelped and then, 'Pull into this lay-by.'

They pulled in. Jeanne pressed the clutch and Helen shifted into neutral. 'A team effort is called for,' Helen said. 'When I say "clutch", lift your foot off the accelerator and press the clutch with your other foot. When I say "OK", do the opposite. Now drive on and turn left into the roundabout. I'll point to where we leave it and which lane to take. All right?'

'I think so,' Jeanne said bravely.

After that they managed almost well. Helen, from the passenger seat, operated the gear lever, directed the route and called every change of speed and lane. The traffic signs and signals were on the unfamiliar side for Jeanne, so Helen accepted the additional duty of reading them. Working as a team, they made it to Bracken House by late afternoon. A further phone call had ensured that there would be extra food in the house and beds aired. Jeanne met and fell for the dogs, admired the house and prepared a quick meal for three from the available ingredients. Her approval of the available wines was qualified.

Once again proceeding by teamwork, they called at David's cottage and collected his mail, the few books and the laptop computer that he wanted to have with him. Helen wondered what the staff would say to the accumulation of goods and chattels around him, but she decided that the nursing staff at least would be eating out of his hand by now. She called up and printed his few emails.

They still had time to catch the end of the evening visiting hours. The light was going. By now, Jeanne was learning the feel of the car and could even find her way through the gear changes, but she had difficulty with the dipswitch. Helen took over control of the headlights and they made it to the hospital without disaster. David was still confined to bed but looking, Helen thought, much more comfortable than on her previous visit. She noticed that the on-demand painkiller had been removed. They touched cheeks.

'I have brought Jeanne to meet you,' Helen said. 'You spoke to her on the phone, remember?'

Jeanne asked him how he was. David said that he could never have forgotten that voice, but that she sounded tall and dark, not small and blonde. He added that he was not disappointed.

Jeanne stooped and kissed him on each cheek, twice. David, who had been brought up familiar with the language of France but not its customs, looked surprised but gratified. Jeanne's English, though precise, was halting and laborious, so they were soon chattering in French.

'They're going to get me on my feet soon,' David said, 'and then I should almost be ready to go home. They send a physiotherapist to keep my muscles working. You understand "physiotherapist"?' he asked Jeanne. 'I don't know the French for it.'

137

'Without doubt,' Jeanne said. 'But if I get my hands on you, you will soon feel better.'

David looked anxiously at Helen again. 'Jeanne is a masseuse,' Helen explained quickly.

'Then I believe you.'

They discussed David's present and probable progress for some minutes, with only occasional halts to close minor gaps between the two languages. Through the open door, Helen spotted the elderly doctor whom she had found to be sympathetic. She darted outside and caught him between visits. He seemed happy to take a break in the little side-room. He even produced coffee. 'Your grandson is showing a real talent for mending,' he said. 'He has no internal injuries and his concussion has passed off. We'll have to see how his legs feel when we let him try them. As soon as he can manage with crutches, you can have him back, but he'll have to visit regularly as an outpatient. The only thing wrong with him now is the usual one. Boredom. We haven't seen you here for a few days.'

Helen refused to feel guilty. 'I'm in France

just now,' she said. 'Business. I'm only here for a day or two but I hope to finish over there soon. I've brought a young lady to visit him.'

'So I noticed. Quite biblical,' said the doctor, 'comforting him with virgins.'

'Between you and me, I think that that may be what she really is. A virgin, I mean. There aren't many of them left, but some of the French middle classes are still very straight-laced. Listen.' They listened. The sound of laughter could be heard from the direction of David's room. 'I hope they aren't disturbing the other patients.'

The doctor smiled. 'That,' he said, 'is exactly what this place needs a little more of. And your grandson in particular.'

'That is just what I had in mind. He lives too reserved and monastic a life even when he's well, although between you and me he does kick over the traces with the wrong sort of girl from time to time.'

The doctor seemed amused. 'And this is the right sort of girl?'

'We shall see what we shall see. We will have to go back to France on Sunday morning. Only for a few days, I hope. Will we be restricted to visiting hours tomorrow?'

'I'll have a word with the ward sister.'

They spoke for a little longer. Helen was surprised to realize that they were actually flirting. Encountering Jules again seemed to have set her calendar back. When she returned to David's room he was lying face down on the bed. He was nude and making noises suggesting extreme pleasure as Jeanne kneaded his buttocks.

It had been made very clear that, however much blind-eye-turning might have been requested, they would not be welcomed, or even admitted, next day before the normal hour for morning visits. That left them with a little time in hand when they rose the next day. While the house-and-dog-sitter was taking the dogs for their accustomed walk and Helen gathered up the various items that she might require in order to put her maturing plan into action, Jeanne insisted on making the beds and dusting the whole house.

There was still time for a visit to David's

house. When Jeanne, in the process of (un-invited) doing David's laundry, came across the defaced photograph, she was so incens-ed that if Monsieur Lemaître-Laroque had made a sudden appearance she would certainly have done him an injury. With her muscles toned and her knowledge of anatomy stoked by her profession, Helen thought that she would probably make a worthy attempt at tearing him limb from limb. Such a man, Jeanne said, deserved the worst that Madame Hélène could invent.

At the hospital, David was very clean and tidy, tucked in neatly and with his posses-sions fitted tightly into his bedside locker in a three-dimensional jigsaw puzzle. He had been allowed to retain one book to read. 'It was in case the matron – they called her the Senior Nursing Officer, of all the stupid jargon – made one of her snap inspections. I told them that I wouldn't let Matron smack their bottoms. One of them called me a spoilsport, but that's all the reaction I got.'

'Do you want everything out of your locker again?' Helen asked.

'Thanks, Gran. But we'd better wait until

the nurses have gone on their weekend razzle. You go back to France tomorrow? I'll miss you.'

He was looking at Jeanne as he spoke but Helen chose to interpret his words as referring to herself. 'Your friend Lemaître has an appointment with Jeanne the next day. We have to be ready.'

David sobered quickly. 'Don't think I'm not grateful. But have you worked out yet what you're going to do? For instance, do you really think that you can follow him home? A con man who's eternally suspicious? He'd spot a car behind him in a minute.'

'My dear boy, you do me less than justice. During my years investigating all the powerful miscreants in the world, it was often necessary to listen – highly illegally – to what was being said on telephones or behind closed doors. I had a very good relationship with a firm that develops that sort of goods – I believe it isn't illegal to make or own them in Britain, only to use them. Their director is retired now but he could still do an old friend a favour. I received a package this morning, containing a magnetic homing bug that I'll attach to his car on Monday while Jeanne deals with his fibrosis and plants a carefully prepared story.'

'You're amazing,' David said. 'I never believed that you'd find the man. But what do you intend to do about him?'

Helen hesitated. Then she shrugged. 'All right. I'll tell you the tale. We can use the time to thrash out the details and to rehearse Jeanne in her role. Settle down, children. Are you sitting comfortably?'

Far from sitting comfortably, Helen got up, looked up and down the corridor and then closed the door. 'I wouldn't want a single word of this to get out,' she said. For twenty minutes she spoke steadily, laying out her plan in logical order. They were speaking in French, so she went slowly for David's sake. When she finished, all three were laughing. David complained that laughing still hurt his ribs.

'But will he really buy it?' David said. 'It's ingenious but it does seem a bit of a cliché.'

'If he doesn't, we can start again; and at

least we should know where he lives. But I think he'll buy it. In fact, I'm sure of it. All confidence tricks boil down to the same basic formula. Somebody is offered something of great value and finds that he's bought little or nothing. I've known a few rogues in my professional life and they're the easiest to fool because they're always looking for the quick and easy return. He'll believe it, in fact, because he'll want to believe it. And remember, clichés are only clichés because they're true.'

'He'll want assurances.'

'I'm making arrangements.'

After a pause, David nodded. 'All right, let's put flesh on the bones.'

They settled down to polishing the story. Jeanne, it was soon clear, had the makings of a very competent actress. ('Damn it!' David said in English. 'She's convincing *me* and I know that she's fibbing!') When David's lunch arrived, the two ladies ate in the café beside the entrance hall. When they returned, he had been tucked in again and his property returned to the locker.

By Sunday morning, David's French had

improved to the point of comparative fluency and Jeanne was taking pains with her English. The time for *au revoir* arrived. 'And *bon chance,*'said David.

'You do not say *bon chance,*' said Jeanne.

'In some circles, that is like saying "Good luck" in the theatre,' Helen explained. 'You say *"Merde".*'

'But that's rude, isn't it?' David protested.

'It doesn't have quite the same implication as the English equivalent. If somebody stood up in public and said "Excretion" or "Dung", you wouldn't be shocked, would you?'

'I suppose not,' David said. He sounded less than certain.

Eleven

They had to hurry to return the car and catch the afternoon plane. They changed planes twice, but the waits were very short. As they crossed the French coast Jeanne said thoughtfully, 'I prefer the Englishman at home.'

'You mean that you would prefer him to stay at home?'

Jeanne giggled and then sobered. 'No. Well, perhaps. What I meant,' she said seriously, 'was that the English who settle in the Dordogne bring money and employment, but they only come because they can buy houses cheaply and they like the weather, the climate. Many of them do not even try to learn the language and they treat us without manners.'

'Not many nations like being judged by

146

their expatriates,' Helen said. 'I have noticed, in many parts of the world, that anyone
with pride in his own country must consider
all others to be his inferior.'

'Feeling superior is natural,' said Jeanne,
'but one should have the good manners to
conceal it.'

At Bergerac, Helen's own car was waiting,
neither stolen nor vandalized but roasting in
the sunshine. They stood in shade while
they waited for the air conditioning to make
the car habitable. 'I shall be glad to leave the
driving to you,' Jeanne said. 'Driving on the
wrong side of the road with everything back
to front I found most difficult.'

'That is how I feel over here,' said Helen.
'I wish to overtake this lorry; tell me if the
road is clear. Thank you. But I should tell
you that this is the wrong side of the road.
England adopted traffic on the left because
that is the best side for a right-handed man
wearing a sword to mount his horse. The
rest of the world would have followed but
Napoleon, because he hated England so
much, determined to do everything differ-
ently. We won't change, because we know

we're doing it right, so if the rest of the world wants uniformity it can change back.'

'Typical,' Jeanne said, but her voice was shaking with laughter. 'I begin to agree with Napoleon.'

A surprise was waiting for them at the Hotel Marmande. Helen had turned back to check that the car's sunroof was slightly open for purposes of ventilation, an act for which she was to be profoundly thankful – if she and Jeanne had entered together, her plan would have required drastic revision. As she turned back again towards the imposing four sets of double doors, Jeanne was just entering. She saw the girl hesitate and then walk on, raising a hand in greeting. The gesture could have been casual and yet, in that subliminal way by which we read each other's body language, she was sure that the gesture was intended in part as a warning to her.

She re-entered the car. Why would a warning have been necessary? The police could hardly be lying in wait; she had not yet offended against the law. Could it be that

Janine had sold them out and that Laroque had brought some hard men to warn them off? Years earlier, after an unexpectedly revealing interview with an African dictator, she had learned the value of being ready for a quick departure. She started the engine of her car and waited. At least the outlook could have been worse. The hotel garden was bright with marguerites, irises and pansies and fragrant with mock orange.

The air conditioning was just renewing its blessedly cool stream of air into the car when Jeanne came out again and headed in her direction. At least the girl did not look particularly distressed. Helen unlocked her own door, thereby unlocking the others, and Jeanne lowered herself into the passenger's seat.

'Laroque,' she said. 'Or Lemaître, but he has registered as Laroque.'

'That seems to be his local name,' Helen said, 'possibly his real one. I think we should stick to it. What about him? Is he here?'

'He was at the desk as I reached the doors. I had to walk on or it would have looked strange. I was still wondering whether he would expect me to remember him when he looked at me and said, "Ah, Mademoiselle Boutet, I think I have an appointment with you for tomorrow." I greeted him politely and said that it was probably so but that I hadn't checked my diary. I said that I hoped he would forgive me if I asked him to remind me of his name.'

Helen looked around. All the hotel's car parking was visible from where she sat. There was an impressive display of expensive cars winking in the sun, but no E-type Jaguar. 'That was good thinking,' she said, 'but did he say why he was here?'

'Oh yes. He was in a talkative mood. I sensed that he felt out of place and needed someone to talk to. He said that he had fallen out with his lady friend and she was being noisy and aggressive. So he had moved everything that he valued into the garage and locked it up, and he had decided that he was seeing me tomorrow so he might as well treat himself to a little luxury for the one night and then go home tomorrow when I had loosened his muscles. And if she has not left the house by then she will be very sorry.' Jeanne laughed grimly. 'That I can believe. There are angry scratches on his face and he does not seem to me to be the sort of man whom one can scratch with impunity. All the same, it seemed to me that he was hiding a secret smile, as if he had already given some punishment.' Jeanne shivered.

'But he still did not give you any hint where the house is?'

'No, Madame.'

'I think it is high time that you called me Hélène. But for the moment we should not be seen together.' Jeanne put her hand to the door-latch. 'In here is safe,' Helen assured her. 'In this light, nobody will see faces through these dark windows. Do you know which is his car?'

'No, Hélène. I have no way of knowing.'

'If Marcel is on the desk, perhaps you could look in the register.'

'But in France hotel guests are not asked for their car numbers.'

'How very strange.' Helen considered the problem. 'I shall wait here in case he comes out. I must know his car if I am to put the homing device in it. But men of his stamp hate to leave behind them a trail that others may follow. You go back inside and phone your friend Janine. She may at least be able to describe the car. Then phone me on my mobile and tell me the result. You have time to do that?'

Jeanne looked at her watch and nodded. 'Understood.' Jeanne quitted the car and walked steadily into the hotel. Helen settled down to wait. She checked that her cellphone was switched on and then found a radio station broadcasting a clarinet concerto by Louis Spohr. If she could not track Laroque to his lair, part of her plan would work; but the other part ... Guests were coming and going but not one of them was her quarry. Waiting had comprised a large part of her working life. Despite her anxiety, she had to fight against sleep.

The jingle from her cellphone brought her to alertness. 'I spoke with Janine. She thinks that his car was large, and it was silver or some pale colour. She does not know about cars,' Jeanne said with a sniff.

Helen made a face. That description

would have covered half the cars within view.

She waited again. She had always been in the habit of keeping paper and pencils in her car. She noted down the registration numbers of every arrival, for purposes of elimination. When the music had reached the rondo she only had three numbers noted. How could a busy hotel survive without knowing the registration numbers of guests' cars? Suppose that one of them had boxed another in ... But the car park was large and the parking well disciplined. This was going to take for ever. Many of the cars might belong to residents who had settled in for a visit of several days. Some would belong to visitors who had only come to dine or to make use of other facilities, or perhaps to meet a lover. Patiently, she noted down the number of every car present. Last thing at night would be the time to return. Some of the cars would have departed. Others would be newly arrived. Of the rest ... perhaps she would think of something. For the moment her mind was blank.

She finished listing the registration numbers and entered the hotel, reclaimed her key and went to her room for a bath and a rest.

Most of the guests dressed up for dinner, so she selected a formal dress in dark blue silk. When she went for dinner, the dining room was becoming crowded. The head waiter apologized. There was a conference in the hotel, he said, for that day only. Laroque, she saw, was alone at a table for two. The head waiter led her in that direction. Helen waited until they were within earshot. 'I would rather have a table to myself.'

'Alas, Madame, impossible unless Madame is prepared to wait. Perhaps in half an hour...'

'Well, I must eat.' Laroque looked up and met her eye. 'So,' she said, 'I suppose we must make the best of it.'

He half rose. 'I shall consider myself to have quite the best of it.'

And this, she thought, was the man who had drawn on her photograph with disgustingly fertile imagination. She bowed austerely.

She made her selection. There were extra waiters on duty. Her hors d'oeuvre arrived quickly. They ate in silence. She tried to catch the eye of the wine waiter but he was busy attending to the conference delegates. Laroque had an opened bottle of Monbazillac beside him. Evidently he decided that good manners required him to make the gesture if he was to melt into his background. He lifted the bottle. 'Madame will join me?'

She hesitated for what she judged to be the right interval. 'You are kind. Thank you.'

'Not at all.' He filled her glass. She raised the glass with a tiny gesture that he might have taken for a toast and took a sip. The sweet wine was out of place, but it would come into its own later in the meal. Laroque was already on to his dessert course. Confident that he could soon escape, he asked politely, 'You have come far, Madame?'

'I live near Paris now. But I was brought up near here. My husband died last year and I decided to visit the places that I knew in my youth and see if any of my old friends are still alive.'

He made a small, wordless sound of sympathy. 'And are they, Madame?'

'Not that I have so far discovered. And you?'

'Not far. I have decorators in and I wished for a night or two away from the smell of paint. You will excuse me?' He rose, bowed politely and left the dining room.

Helen sent a venomous look at his unsuspecting back. He could have saved her a lot of trouble by saying where he lived. On the other hand, knowing the nature of the man, he would almost certainly have given her a false pointer and had her wasting her time, searching in quite the wrong direction.

After dinner, by arrangement, she met Jeanne and Jules in her room. She had again ensured that drinks were provided. It was the first time that Jules had been introduced to the details of Helen's master plan. He quite understood his part and, chuckling, he said that he would be delighted. They spent some time in refining the scheme, Helen playing the part of the trickster and trying to detect flaws in the stories presented by the others.

There would, Jules said, be a poetic justice about the denouement if it succeeded. He had been enjoying the very good brandy provided by the hotel at Helen's request, and he was becoming expansive. 'There is something to be savoured when the biter is bitten. I will tell you a story.' His face lit and for a moment Helen was reminded of the wicked twinkle that she had last seen in a barn, more than half a century earlier. 'Two years ago a man came to our warehouse. He is in business in a big way and he was considering a large investment in machinery for the many farms managed by his firm. He put us to a great deal of work and some expense. He accepted several good lunches and dinners, but we thought that money well invested. Then, during what we thought to be the last meeting before the order being signed, his assistant arrived and the man went out to confer with him, leaving his cell-phone on the table. My youngest son, who was not in the meeting, came in to tell us that he had just received a call from a friendly manufacturer to warn us that the man had no intention of placing such a large order with us but was letting us help him to finalize all the specifications before negotiating to purchase direct from the factories. He was to meet them that same afternoon.'

'A dirty trick,' Helen remarked, 'but it happens all the time.'

'That does not make it better. However, one of my sons took the man's cellphone away to the toilet and he replaced the ringing jingle with quite a different noise. You can guess? You are not shocked, Hélène?'

'No,' Helen said, 'I am not shocked.' There had been episodes in her life that would probably have shocked Jules.

Jules was speaking with difficulty, rocking with laughter. 'Just when he would have been meeting the manufacturers, my son called his mobile number. The call was answered but the voices at the other end were not saying quite what one would expect...'

A little later, Jules rose to go. He was slightly unsteady. Helen looked at Jeanne. 'I think perhaps that you should drive your great-uncle home. I will follow in my car and bring you back.'

Jules protested but he was overruled. The motorcycle police were at their most officious during the night. On the pretext of testing its comfort, he elected to travel in Helen's car rather than in his own, but it was soon evident that that was not his real motive.

Helen was neither shocked nor embarrassed by a hand on her leg and the murmuring of suggestions that were undoubtedly provocative. Sex, she still thought, should in theory not switch off at a given age. Perhaps it was truly sad that it was often allowed to lapse, most commonly because of the embarrassment of arriving at a *modus operandi* with a new partner. Jules, of course, was not exactly a new partner, but they had not shared intimacies for nearly sixty years. Her body was still trim but she could not delude herself into thinking that it still had any of its old firmness or bounce. She pushed his hand away and told him, quite kindly, to behave himself. On the other hand, of course, it was good to be asked. Few women resent being desired. She even felt another small stirring of the old attraction, but at an emotional rather than a physical level.

When Jeanne and Helen returned they had to move the car only once in order to check every number plate in the car park. Some cars had left, others had arrived. There were still sixteen cars not accounted for, three of them large and pale.

'I do not think that this man will be easy to follow,' Helen said, 'but if we can not find the car I shall have to try. I shall look again in the morning, but I quite expect that some of the cars belong to ladies who have come to join lovers and who do not wish to seen leaving. I see that I shall have to be up and about at an early hour and pray that most of the cars have left before you have finished Monsieur Laroque's massage.'

'It is a pity,' Jeanne said. 'Your so beautiful plan upset by such an unhappy chance.'

'Perhaps the gods do not wish us to succeed.'

As if the gods chose that moment to prove her wrong, the hotel doors opened and extra lights came on. A figure descended the steps, even by that poor light unmistakably the figure of the man who had defrauded David. He crossed to a white or pale grey Audi, collected something from the boot, re-locked the car and walked quickly back into the hotel. Thirty seconds later the homing bug was in place.

Twelve

Helen would dearly have loved to eavesdrop on Jeanne and Laroque during his massage. She could have assured her that all was going in accordance with her plan or, if there was any deviation from her script, telephoned Jeanne with advice or instructions. But there was no possible way that this could be arranged with the hairdressing salon next door in full swing. There was always the danger that Jeanne might arouse his suspicions and that David had been mistaken in supposing that Laroque was not a man of violence, so with a vague intent of being near enough to render some sort of help, she booked an appointment with the hairdresser, timing it early in the hope of being finished at about the time that Jeanne finished the massage.

Her timing, however, was off. The sole hairdresser turned out to be very thorough and a slow and talkative worker. While the massage took place next door, Helen was under a very noisy hair drier and would not have heard a sound even if Jeanne next door had been dismembered with a chainsaw. By the time that she escaped, beautifully coiffed but simmering with impatience, Laroque had departed. Jeanne was already engaged w   next client and, when Helen looked   the door, could only signal helplessn   by means of raised eyebrows and a very quick shrug. Helen's only consolation was that she had received a modish haircut which, she thought, took years off her.

She had already had a reminder of how chance can upset the best-laid plans. She judged it more urgent than waiting for Jeanne's account to see whether Laroque's car was gone and, if so, to follow it up before the battery in the homer ran out, the vehicle disappeared into a tunnel or Laroque parted with it. Helen visited her room to collect

the bag in which she had gathered everything that experience suggested she might
need.

The presence of the satellite navigation
unit had made the installation of the homing bug very much easier. The unit installed
in Helen's car was the latest and best of its
kind, short of military technology. Instead
of focusing on the bug under Laroque's rear
wing, it sent a question to a satellite far
overhead. The satellite knew the present
position of Laroque's car and relayed it to
the unit that Helen had just switched on.
That unit then presented it both as a readout of the latitude and longitude but also by
way of the arrow on a rotating card con-
trolled by a tiny computer. There were none
of the hesitations, sudden switches on to an
echo signal or limitations of range to which
earlier units were prone.

Laroque's car had indeed gone, and when
she switched on the unit the arrow was
pointing in the general direction of Liverac.
Helen let out a sigh of relief so deep that it
made her head swim. She brought herself
under control and set out in pursuit. She

had no need for undue hurry – the last thing she wanted was to meet Laroque returning from some side-trip. Even so, the unit was so easy to follow that she needed only an occasional glance down, and could pay attention to her driving while watching for any sign of the Audi parked at the road-side. She could ignore the many hamlets; Laroque would not want to live cheek by jowl with inquisitive neighbours, although her fear was that he might have opted for the anonymity of a block of flats with the Jaguar in a lockup nearby ... if, and this was a fear that nagged at her constantly, if he had not already sold it. She could only bank on the lust of the true enthusiast. If he ran true to form, he would want to own it, at least for a while, before selling it on.

Only when she arrived at a fork in the minor, rural road, to find the arrow on the card pointing between the two branches, was it necessary for her to stop, get out the map and compare it with the readout. The map reference being quoted in the LCD display was no longer changing. A glance at the map showed a twist of the right-hand branch, explaining the anomalous reading of the arrow. Her quarry had come to a halt.

She set off cautiously on the right-hand limb of the fork, which soon curved to the left around the flank of a low hill. The French countryside is well sprinkled with dwellings. Passing another such house, she glanced down, as had become her habit, but this time to see the card rotating. She snatched a quick glance and was given a glimpse of a silver car beside the door. That was enough. She drove on, to where a wood half a kilometre ahead was draped on the skyline. Over the crest and out of view from the house, a track left the road and she could pull off for a moment of consideration. When she thought back, she was sure that she had not betrayed her interest by any hesitation of the car.

The map was very helpful, but it could not offer her an easy alternative route back to the hotel. She preferred not to pass the house again too soon, in case Laroque was on the lookout. She marked the position of the house on the map and jotted down the map reference. The house had, as she expected, not been part of a hamlet, but was one of the individual houses that occurred, even under Napoleonic law, when a son of the deceased farmer preferred to build in the fields. It was not small. Recalling it from her early days in France, she thought that it had been added to over the years and that she remembered a garage.

He might only be visiting. She pulled the car forward until it was out of sight from the road. She changed her shoes for a pair of stout brogues. She had provided herself with a loose, thin silk blouse of dark grey and she pulled it on over her white jumper. Feeling less conspicuous, she hung her lightweight Zeiss binoculars round her neck, locked the car carefully and picked her way to the edge of the wood. A swell of the ground cut off most of her view, but further from the road and still near the edge of the wood, she saw a ladder leading up a tree. The sudden provision of just what she most needed seemed magical until she realized that she had found the ladder to the 'high seat' where in England some hunter would have been in the habit of waiting to surprise roe deer. In the Dordogne, he would be more likely to lie in wait for wild boar. She decided not to worry about her clothes but to take great care of her person. At such an age, a fall is no laughing matter. Clothes can be replaced without surgery, but damaged joints can not. She pulled herself carefully from one rough rung to another.

The 'high seat' was no more than a plank between two limbs of the tree. Another timber had presumably been intended as a steadying support for a rifle, but for Helen it made a secure backrest. She sat with the smell of foliage all around her, and in her ears the sound of a light breeze rattling the leaves. She found that she was looking at Laroque's house, one long stubble-field away, through a lacework of green. She studied the shape of the house and the layout of its garden with care, although, in typically French fashion, the house was half lost behind a screen of shrubs, poplars and fruit trees. If Laroque did not drive off shortly, her next visit might have to be at night.

Laroque was not so obliging. There was little breeze and not even the sound of traffic disturbed the quiet. The windows of the house were open. For a short period, Helen heard music as from a radio or hi-fi. Later came the sound of a woman's voice raised in what sounded like protest. Helen would have liked to listen in, but there was no way to approach the house unseen in daylight and she was too far away to hear clearly. It would be something to follow up at a later date. In the meantime, Jeanne would be free to tell her story by now, and Helen was anxious to hear it.

She climbed down carefully and brushed herself down as well as she could. Backing the car out on to the road had to be accomplished with care. She drove back past the house, carefully making no suspicious variation of her speed but making some more mental notes. A name-board at the gate said Lefische, followed by the house's name, Souvris. The house seemed to have grown around a smaller cottage. The French farmer grudges paying a contractor for work that he could do himself, but the extensions had not been done in the slapdash manner usual when a family turns to for a co-operative effort; they had been carried out with skill and taste, employing local stone and some timber boarding that she thought was probably oak. There was indeed a double garage but the Audi was still stand-ing outside. Either Laroque was going out again, or could it be that the garage was fully occupied?

The house was too fully screened by trees to allow her to spy for electronic alarms. To repass the house might invite Laroque to start wondering. She picked a roundabout route from the map.

At the hotel lunch, even the protracted French lunch, was almost finished. Jules was awaiting her in the hall. She took him to her room and she established by phone that Jeanne was free for the next hour. She called Room Service and ordered coffee, canapés and sandwiches for three.

Jeanne still had some of the appetite pecu-liar to the young. To allow her time to satisfy the direst of her hunger, Helen called up her

own reserves of patience and led off by
announcing that they now knew where
Laroque had headed when he left the hotel.
She described the house, its location and
environs in some detail. 'I think we can
assume that he lives there. According to the
board at his gate, he calls himself Lefische,'
she said. 'But if we keep changing every
time he adopts another alias we're going to
muddle ourselves. We'll stay with Laroque.'

When she judged that Jeanne could survive for a half hour, she said, 'Now, child. I
see that you also are bursting with news. Tell
all, missing nothing out. But first, you think
that he took the bait?'

'I think so, Hélène.'

'Good! Now I can listen with my mind at
peace.'

Jeanne popped one last mushroom canapé
into her mouth, chewed and swallowed. *'Eh
beh!* As you suggested, Hélène, I left him
in the room for a few minutes. When I
returned he had the decoration in his hands.
We had rearranged the room a little,' she
explained to her great-uncle, 'so that there
was only one place of interest, and there

we placed certain of Madame Hélène's souvenirs of the Resistance. In particular there was an iron cross, set in a polished block of acrylic resin.'

'I did not believe that any man of his profession could be left alone in a room without examining its contents,' Helen explained. 'Curiosity would be an essential part of the confidence trickster's makeup.'

'But I remember that iron cross,' Jules said. 'We took it off a German who was killed by a grenade.'

Like many another who is feeling the passage of the years, Helen's short-term memory was liable to lapses but events of half a century earlier remained crystal clear. 'He was only wounded,' she said. 'Pierre killed him later.'

Jeanne flinched but resumed her story. 'I told him, as you said, that my great-uncle had taken it off a German who he had killed during the attack on the famous train. A minute later, when I had him on the table and I was starting work on his back muscles, he asked what famous train. I stayed very close to the truth, because he might check up. He might even already have known some of the story. I said that the Resistance had word of a northbound train drawing, among its other wagons, one filled with the Germans' plunder from the museums and châteaux to the south. As soon as I mentioned plunder, I felt his muscles tense and I knew that I had his full attention. He said that he believed that the south was unoccupied.

'I said that technically this was true but that later on, when it became clear that Germany could not win the war, pillaging occurred further south. I said that he'd have to ask my great-uncle about that. It was decided, I told him, that this train must not leave France and a unit of the Resistance set out to intercept the train by destroying a bridge. My great-uncle was among the men, which is how I know the story so well. Word had reached the Germans and the leader was taken. The band was about to disperse when a young girl, a real heroine of the Resistance, took charge and led the men. The train was stopped and the wagon emptied into a lorry. But they had been too slow overcoming the guards and more Germans arrived. There was much shooting and the Resistance was driven off.'

'That much at least was true,' Helen said. 'Apart from the heroine, that is.'

'I stayed with the truth, as you told me. He was trying to relax but I knew, through my fingertips, that he was very much interested. He said that he supposed that the Germans recovered all the treasure. I said that they had certainly recovered all the gold and the precious objects and most of the paintings, but there had remained rumours to this day, and now and again the police would again take an interest and start searches and inquiries. Whenever I asked my great-uncle what was the truth I was told a different story every time. He asked me what was the nub of the rumours, and I told him that the most usual was that the Germans had recovered all the loot except for one very valuable painting by Fragonard. This was sealed in a tube and a group of two or three from the Resistance got away with it. It had been the centrepiece of the art gallery in Toulouse. It is still missing, because the police have asked in particular about it.

'That was all until he was about to leave. "Your great-uncle," he said. "He is still alive?" I said that he was and that he and his sons had a business in agricultural machinery not far from here. He pretended to be interested in the machinery and asked the address and I gave him one of the business cards.' Jeanne chuckled. 'I could see that he recognized the name, but he was not going to say that he had once approached the firm in the hope of robbing it.'

'He was truly hooked?' Helen asked.

'I would say so.'

Jules made as if to rise. 'I had better get back. He may be looking for me already.'

'There is no hurry now,' Helen said. 'We can dictate the pace, simply by not meeting him or being reluctant to speak. It will make the story more convincing than if we showed haste. Also it will give him time to make his own enquiries. He will not come to your office, Jules, in case somebody remembers him from the time when he enquired about machinery. I do not think that any of the avenues open to him will give rise to any doubts, but now is the stage at which he will be alert. Later, once he thinks that he is deceiving us, his mind will close to the possibility that we are deceiving him. Tonight I intend to go and study his house and the other venue.'

'I shall come with you?' Jules enquired.

'I should be glad of your company.'

When the other two had gone, Helen lay down on her bed and drew sleep over her like a blanket. She had been missing her afternoon naps recently and she would be lucky to see her bed that night much before dawn.

Thirteen

The small hours of the following morning saw Jules driving his Citroën, with Helen at his side. On the back seat rested two canvas bags holding a selection of the gadgets collected during a career divided between reporting from the more turbulent parts of the world and winkling out the carefully hoarded secrets of the great but not so good. She had added her favourite walking stick. There was no way of knowing how far she might have to walk, but she did know that her joints were likely to start protesting after the first mile or two.

Bats and nocturnal insects flickered in the headlamps. A rotund badger scuttled across the road. Rabbits with no traffic sense seemed determined to die under the wheels.

Helen had the map unfolded on her knee. She had studied it before they set off, so that she only needed an occasional blink of a small torch. 'We go the very long way round,' she said. 'If the sound of our departure in the silence of the night causes him to wonder, that is acceptable. But if our arrival alerts him, that could spell disaster.'

'*Entendu*,' Jules said. 'The moon is coming out. That may help us.'

'Perhaps a little bit. I have a night vision monocular in one of my bags but it works even better with a little help from the moon. I want first to see what lights and sensors he has outside the house before making an approach.'

'That is sensible. We do not enter the house?'

'Certainly not!' Helen sounded shocked. 'You know what a noise these old French houses make. We do not enter anywhere at all except the garden. I want to look through the side window into the garage, to see if he is keeping my grandson's Jaguar there. If not, then we have a new problem. Does he keep it somewhere else? And where? Or has he already disposed of it? I may have to think of a new twist, to find out, but first we look in the obvious place.'

'Now I understand,' Jules said humbly.

Any crow gifted with an adequate sense of direction need have covered only a little over thirty kilometres to do the journey. By road, forty would have sufficed, but in order to approach the track where Helen had stopped earlier without first passing the house, they had nearly sixty kilometres to travel. The roads were good, however, and there was no traffic, so they covered the distance in little over an hour.

They entered the track without using lights and with the engine no more than idling. The sound of the cicadas and the toads plip-plopping, along with the slight breeze blowing from the house to the wood, should ensure that they were not heard. She refrained from reminding Jules to close the car's door silently – in her experience, nothing would annoy a man more than being given obvious advice or being told to do that which he was going to do anyway. To her relief, he eased it closed with no more than a faint click. The night-time scents and sounds of the countryside enveloped them.

On her earlier visit, she had noted a path, probably made by wild boar, across the stubble field towards a rear corner of Laroque's garden. They followed it until they had the front and one side of the house in view through a gap in the trees, and stopped while Helen used her night vision monocular. Aided by the moon, it showed the detail of the house with remarkable clarity. Laroque's Audi was again standing on the gravel. 'Two sensor-lights to the front of the house,' she said softly at last. 'No other sensors that I can see. Let's go. If the lights come on suddenly, either hide or slip away.' She leaned on his arm, only partly to guide him. Her medication was keeping her arthritis under control, but there was no denying that she was becoming very stiff. The contact was both friendly and comforting.

They found a gate at the corner of the garden. It was bolted, but Jules managed to work the bolt free. Easing the gate very slowly, they managed to open it without undue noise. 'You stay here,' she muttered. She slipped off her shoes. The paths were of sharp gravel, but at least on the gravel a soft foot was quieter than a harder shoe. A few paces between the overgrown bushes brought her to the side window of the garage. She produced her torch and shaded it carefully with her hands. A small and modest Fiat was in front of her – for use, she guessed, when Laroque wished to melt into a middle-class background. And beyond the Fiat was a low shape that had to be the E-type Jaguar.

Warmth and the sound of breathing beside her made her look round. Jules, similarly unshod, had joined her. He put his lips to her ear. 'It is very beautiful,' he said. He seemed to be referring to the Jaguar. Helen felt that it was fair comment.

'Could you manage that lock?' she asked him softly. She shone the torch on the inside of the garage door.

One glance at the rim-lock sufficed. 'With a toothpick,' Jules whispered.

The house had seemed silent but suddenly there were sounds. Helen jumped and prepared to run before realizing that the sounds were nothing to do with her. A woman's voice was raised and this time there could be no doubt that it was in protest. Then the voice died away and Helen could just make out the sound of weeping. She felt the skin on her scalp tighten. It might be no more than a domestic tiff over money or the arrangement of the furniture, but something in the timbre of the voice suggested desperation. It went against the grain to ignore the suggestion of abuse, but any form of interference at this stage would have been madness.

Nor was this the time to enjoy her gains. They began to retrace their steps very carefully. Helen would most have liked to disable the E-type so that it would be available when she wanted it, but she could not risk triggering Laroque's suspicions if he should decide to start the car.

They were almost at the gate when she brushed against something that slid with a rustling of undergrowth and hit the ground with a crackle of twigs. Jules took hold of the gate but Helen remembered the stiffness of the hinges. Sudden opening would make an unmistakable squeal. And it was already too late. The outside lights flashed on, painting the garden in a stark pattern of black and white. Helen saw that the falling object had been a ladder, left propped against a fruit tree.

The lock at the front door clicked and more light spilled out. They ducked into the deep shadow of a bush. Helen smelled juniper. The bush was barely big enough to hide them both. Through the foliage she saw Laroque's shadow spread across the gravel and then the man himself emerged to stand, poking his head and glaring into the shadows. In his hands was a long firearm – a rifle, or more probably a shotgun, which Helen thought might be worse. They were well within range of a shotgun and the spread of the pattern would increase the danger of a hit.

'Who's there?' Laroque called suddenly. 'I can see you. Come on out or I'll start shooting.'

Helen was almost sure that he was bluffing. Jules must have been in agreement.

They froze. The world was silent. Helen tried to breathe without a sound. She thought that Laroque would hear her heart-beats. After a dozen or more beats, she felt Jules move suddenly. She put out her hand to check him but at the same moment there came another stirring in the undergrowth followed by a snuffling grunt. Laroque raised the shotgun and fired. Pellets rattled through the leaves nearby.

'And don't come back,' Laroque shouted. The door closed. After an interval, the sensor lights switched off.

When they were safely on the stubble they began to replace their shoes – not an easy manoeuvre for an elderly person without anywhere to sit or to put up a foot. She knelt uncomfortably and tied Jules's laces for him with shaking hands. He returned the service. She determined to remonstrate with him for not doing what he was told, but by the time they reached the car she had thought again. A Frenchman does not take lightly to being given orders by a woman.

'We were lucky,' she said. 'That wild boar...'

He smiled so that his teeth shone in the moonlight. Then he repeated the snuffling grunt.

'That was you?' she said. 'And you threw a stone? That was quick thinking.'

Instead of replying, he put his arms around her and drew her close. She was glad of the comfort and he deserved his reward. They kissed, but when it seemed that the old passion was making a return – which, she thought, might just be appropriate even at their age but not in a wood before dawn – she broke it off.

He held the car door for her. They sat still for a calming minute.

'I saw the car,' he said. 'No wonder your David is desolate. It is beautiful.'

'Beauty is not the point,' she said. 'My grandson spent many months working on it and it is his pride and joy. I am not having any thief taking it away from him. But you are right. It has beauty.'

'I should have had such a grandmother,' he said.

She laughed. 'I remember your grand-mother. She would have dismembered anyone who hurt you.'

'Truly? You think so?' He sounded surprised.

'I know it. But she would never have let you see her devotion.'

As she spoke, she was studying her watch. There was still time for her other errand before anyone awoke, which would save them from losing another night's sleep. When they were moving again he said, 'That would have been his woman's voice that we heard.'

'Yes. Jeanne said that he used having fallen out with his lady friend to explain his presence at the hotel.'

'Yet she is still there, and sounding terrified. I am beginning to conceive of a great dislike of this gentleman.'

'I also,' said Helen.

An hour's driving brought them to where a large but unostentatious building stood back from the obscure minor road.

'You'd better stay in the car,' she said. 'And this time I really mean it. If I'm found lurking around I could explain myself more easily that you could.'

Jules chuckled. 'That is true.'

Helen retrieved her walking stick from under her bags and set off uphill. The garden was well planted with bushes but a broad strip of coarse, mown grass edged the driveway and stood out clearly in the moonlight. Her feet were still sore from the gravel. She had to remind herself that if she had had her dogs with her she would have stepped out more eagerly over twice the distance. The journey round the building seemed interminable. Most of the windows were too large and too far off the ground for her purpose, but when she was almost back at the driveway, the grass came to an end at what was evidently a rear entrance with a broad turning-place for delivery vehicles. Here she found a low window, its sill only knee-high from the ground. There were signs that its purpose had once been for the delivery of logs, although there was now a tank for fuel oil in its own enclosure nearby. She fumbled her torch out of her coat pocket and, careful not to spill any light where it might be seen from the building, studied the window. For a moment she was sure that her plan would not work, that the window was too wide and too flimsy; but when she put the torch against the glass and twisted her neck to look down through the glass she saw that the room was empty except for dust and cobwebs and that the floor was a long way, more than two metres, below her.

She took to the grass again and hobbled all the way back to the car. Behind her, lights were already appearing behind windows as the first of the occupants began to rise. 'That will do nicely,' she told Jules.

The hotel was only beginning to stir into life when Jules dropped her at the imposing front doors. Jules, it seemed, was too sleepy to come up with more than the most banal of amorous remarks. The night porter let her in and noted her order that she be left undisturbed until woken at noon with a substantial brunch; and also her request that Jeanne, as soon thereafter as she could be free, attend to give her a massage. The night porter contemplated her retreating back. With any other lady he would have known that she had spent the night in some other bed. Madame Mercier was surely rather past such carryings-on and yet one heard of such things. He rather hoped that when he was of such an age he would still be able to spend the night in a strange bed. But, of course, it was easier for the woman. He decided to dip into his savings and try Viagra.

Helen, unaware of the thoughts that she had aroused, took to her bed and slept tranquilly until a maid arrived with her brunch.

Jeanne found her adequately rested, well fed, bathed, but uncomfortably stiff. 'You walked further than you are used to?' she asked.

'Not so very far,' Helen said, 'but walking over uneven ground is as bad as at least twice as far on a smooth path, and one must use muscles that are never usually used at all.'

'This is true,' Jeanne said. She set to work with an energy that made Helen groan.

When the treatment was finished, Helen rolled over on the bed. 'I feel easier,' she said. 'Thank you, Jeanne. Did anything happen while I slept?'

'Yes indeed, Hélène. Monsieur Laroque paid me a visit while I was between clients.'

Helen nearly sat up but the effort would have been too much. 'Really? Why did you not give me the news straight away?'

'Your need of the massage seemed greater, the news was not about to change. He explained to me that he is a writer and that he is thinking that one should write a fresh history of the Resistance before the last of its heroes have passed on. He wishes a proper introduction to my great-uncle rather than to go and knock on his door. I said that he was very wise, that my uncle would not often speak about the great days in the Resistance and he was tired of being asked about the treasure train. And I said that he takes great pleasure in good food and wines so that, given a good meal, he would almost certainly open up. Well, I did not see why my great-uncle and I should not get a good meal out of it.'

'Opportunist!' Helen said, smiling. 'But you are not bringing him here, I hope?'

'Certainly not! The cuisine is better at the

Boule d'Or and Great-Uncle Jules assures me that the wines are the most superb.'

'Excellent. When the opportunity arrives, I shall remember your advice. You both know the story to tell. And when my name is mentioned...'

'I say that there is a lady with just that name visiting this very hotel at the moment.'

'Perfect!'

'And now, Hélène, my next client will be waiting. Your stiffness is less?'

Helen tentatively moved her legs. 'It is quite gone. Now go and perform the same magic for another client.'

Jeanne left and Helen closed her eyes again. Within a minute, she was asleep.

Fourteen

Next day, Helen had expected to sleep late. But events were beginning to move and she would have to make her own moves to keep ahead of them. She snapped awake not so very long after her usual time. Her subconscious was insisting that if Laroque asked enough questions of enough people, he would be expecting a positive answer; and this he might not receive.

She enjoyed an excellent breakfast. By dint of perseverance and force of personality she had persuaded, almost brainwashed, the dining room staff into satisfying her desire for bacon and eggs, toasted bread and marmalade, however bizarre they might consider those wishes to be. Other British residents were following suit and *Breakfast*

Anglais had begun appearing on the menu, at an exorbitant price. But while she ate, she decided that she had procrastinated for too long.

From her own room, she phoned the Château de Liverac and spoke to an old friend. 'Would this be a good time to visit you?'

The comte's voice was warm. 'Any time would be a good time.'

Remembering the style kept up at the château even in wartime, she took some trouble with her appearance. She refused to be hurried on the journey. These were roads where once she had cycled on errands, real or fictitious, carrying arms or explosives, forged papers, once even a complete copy of a German general's uniform with medals and badges, disguised as a bag of cabbages. According to Jules, there had been some looting during the hectic days of the German retreat, but the château still had its air of prosperity and of being immune to Communist envy. Evidently there was no shortage of money, because the gardens, though smaller than she remembered, were manicured to perfection. The château still had as many turrets.

A manservant came down the steps and opened the car door but the comte himself arrived in time to escort her up the many steps. They touched cheeks and kissed air, twice each side. The fresh-faced boy she had known had matured into a typical Frenchman, complete with a prominent nose, dark hair and an undershot and shadowed jaw. His thin suit was of good cloth and well cut and he walked with a stick. He led her into a large and masculine study, largely booklined. The huge desk was covered with a drift of papers.

Courteous as ever, he held her chair for her before settling behind the desk. 'It is enchanting to see you again,' he said. 'I have always had the fondest memories of you.' He looked round, to be sure that the servant had gone. Even so, he lowered his voice almost to a whisper. 'Even after two wives and eleven mistresses, you remain foremost in my memory. Would it be indiscreet of me to say that you were my first?'

She laughed. He had never been circumspect. 'You were my first, also,' she said.

'That makes a special bond. What, then, can I do for you?'

She looked at the desk. 'I want you to be writing a book.'

'I *am* writing a book.'

'Not about the Resistance?'

He made a dismissive gesture. 'No. I thought of it, but it was made clear to me that much that happened in those days remains obscure, in many cases I would be unlikely to get at the truth and the whole thing is best forgotten. My position with the locals would have suffered. I am writing about the economics of organic farming in today's climate.'

Nobody had ever looked less like a farmer, but she recalled that the old count's estates had covered a great many hectares including some distinguished and modestly profitable vineyards.

'But you could pretend,' she said. 'Nobody knew more about the Resistance than you did. Let me tell you a story.'

The comte was contemplating her legs. She had always had good legs and of all her features they had suffered least from time. She moved her position slightly to improve his view. 'Take as long as you like,' he said.

'Thank you.' She gave him a very brief history of her family and her grandson. She told the story of the fraud perpetrated against David and explained how she had been brought back to that part of the Dordogne.

The comte was scowling. 'You have told the police?'

This was the question that Helen had been dreading. She could only stick to her previous line of argument and hope that it would suffice. 'Not yet,' she said. 'Perhaps never. At the first sign of a *flic*, I would expect him to bolt. Even if they caught him—'

'They would probably only ask for his driving licence,' said the comte. 'There would be endless delays and costs.'

Helen felt her eyebrows going up of their own accord. As a local nobleman and a major landowner, she had expected him to take a right-wing view of law and order. 'I'm too old for all that trouble,' she said.

'Never too old but much too gentle,' he replied. 'I remember the old Hélène Mercier. She would never have waited for them. You only have to have a dozen Euros to rub together,' he said hotly, 'and they pursue you forever for speeding fines, unapproved tree felling, spitting in a ditch or going into a wood for a pee. If you take the car into a town you daren't even stop. The old Hélène would have had no truck with them.'

He was becoming heated. Helen stifled a sigh. If the locals all chose to remember the one person who had been snatched away, in the final moments of the war and before all the controversy could begin, as a sort of female Rambo figure, that might suit her purpose very well.

'I know the man,' she said. 'I want to deal with him myself. I want to recover what was stolen and I wish to expose the man to such ridicule that he will never dare to cheat again. This is what I plan...'

The comte listened carefully. Amusement began to relieve his features. By the end, he had laughed so that he had to dry his eyes. 'But what do you want of me?' he enquired.

'Only ask and you shall have it.'

'A trickster is very wary,' Helen explained. 'He will certainly wish to check on me. But there are no easy and trustworthy sources open to him. So it will be necessary to invent one. The comte in the local château, one whose war record is remembered and who is writing a book about the Resistance, that should carry conviction.'

The comte was laughing again. 'You may rely on me,' he said. 'Let us have a little lunch and then you can rehearse me in my story.'

'Excellent. But first I may use your phone?' She called the Hotel Marmande. Jeanne was between clients. 'When you meet Laroque,' she said, 'you may use the name of the Comte de Liverac at the Château de Liverac. The comte is writing a book about the Resistance.'

'Really?'

'No, not really. But he will confirm our story.'

'How did you persuade—?'

'You have your means of persuasion,' Helen said, 'and I have mine.'

★ ★ ★

She returned to the hotel by late afternoon feeling hot and dusty and a little bit drunk. The count's hospitality had been generous and that of his fat little wife, as typically French as her husband, no less so. Helen was certain that the comtesse was well aware of her husband's former mistresses, including herself, but she seemed to bear no malice and poured the wine with an equally generous hand.

A luxurious bath washed away the fumes of some very good wine, and a leisurely toilet occupied her until she went for an early dinner. After dinner, however, she was ready to burst with impatience. Jules and Jeanne must by now be at dinner with the appalling Laroque but she was sorely tempted to risk the whole venture by driving to the Boule D'Or to observe the diners from a distance and thus reassure herself that all was proceeding to plan. Laroque, for instance, might have seen through the whole ploy and departed for home in a huff, while her co-conspirators were postponing the dread moment of breaking the news to her.

She gave herself a mental shake for thinking nonsense.

She took to her room, sipped a small brandy, stretched out on her bed, went through her relaxation exercises and, to her later surprise, dozed off. She awoke with a jerk to the sound of a light tapping on the door. She got up and admitted Jeanne. At first glance, the young masseuse looked satisfied.

'Come, sit and talk,' Helen said. 'Give me every detail. But first ... he took the bait?'

Jeanne seated herself neatly, as always. 'We believe so. Unless he is a very good actor. He showed no signs of disbelief.'

'A trickster would have to be a good actor,' Helen said.

'Not as good as this one would have to be,' Jeanne said positively.

Helen felt an uplifting of the heart. Perhaps it would all work out. She gave Jeanne a Grand Marnier from the minibar. She mixed a very dilute brandy and soda for herself and rolled it around her mouth to remove the taste of sleep. 'Go on,' she said. 'Tell all.'

'Very well.' Jeanne sipped delicately from her glass and looked up at the ceiling. 'We were early but he was already at the bar when we entered. He knew me, of course, and I introduced him to my great-uncle. He was a good host, I must say that for him. A table was waiting and we took our drinks to it.

'He proceeded slowly and gently, like a fisherman luring a trout.'

'That is how a skilled trickster would proceed,' Helen said. 'The fly dropped gently on the water. A little twitch to interest the fish. Then movement, suggesting that the fly will escape. Then, when the fly is taken, one good pull sets the hook.' That was exactly how she had lured a concupiscent film star into an in-depth interview.

'I do not think that he is a fisherman,' Jeanne said seriously, 'except for foolish people who will trust him with their money. Between ordering the meal and during the hors d'oeuvres, he kept us chatting about current affairs – nothing heavy, you understand, though I could judge that he leans to the left, but the more amusing topics, show business, scandals, sport, all the lighter topics of the day. With the entrée he introduced the subject of the Resistance and explained his desire to collect material for a book before the anecdotes were lost. He had tact enough not to say "while those who know them are still alive". Great-Uncle Jules had had a few drinks but he kept himself well in hand. Monsieur Laroque put a small tape recorder in front of him and Uncle Jules spoke confidently to it. He produced many tales that I had not heard before and I think that he took pains to mention your name more than once.

'With the sweet course came the oh-so-subtle reference to the incident of the train – which, Laroque pointed out, I had mentioned to him. Great-Uncle Jules, you may know, has a very hard head but if I had not known him so well I would have believed that he was slightly drunk. He hummed and hawed and then he told the story, just as we agreed it. He used your name, telling how you took over command of the group. It was the whole truth and he spoke about the fighting that led to the recapturing of the treasure by the Germans. He finished by saying how the Germans had taken reprisals.

'Monsieur Laroque looked mildly disappointed. "I had heard," he said, without looking at me, "that not all the treasure was recovered. I quite understand that it would be wrong to embarrass any of those who were present during that adventure, but it would also be wrong to let such a gallant story die altogether. If you tell me about it, I will promise to be discreet about the identities of the men and women concerned and not to reveal the hiding place."

'Great-Uncle Jules said that he couldn't reveal the hiding place anyway. He said that it was true that three people had escaped with a package that he believed, from the questions asked by the Germans and later by the gendarmes, contained a very valuable painting by Fragonard. He himself had been one of the three. The driver of the small van that they had borrowed from a farmer said that he knew of a hiding place that would be absolutely safe and that even if it were ever found would have no connection with any one of them. Great-Uncle Jules, because he had some experience in the building trades, went into a large building with Gaston Duprée, the driver, and they removed a loose board from a staircase and hid the package there. When the board was replaced, he said, nobody would ever have known that it could be moved.

'"But where is this building?" Monsieur Laroque asked.

'My great-uncle said that he had not the least idea. "I had been travelling in the back," he said, "and it was as much as I could do to save myself from being buried under turnips and potatoes. Gaston, who had been driving, knew the building because he had at one time been in charge of the maintenance of several colleges and suchlike; but he took part in an attack on a German guard post a few days later and was killed for his pains. I had told the old fool that it was a bad plan and the results would not be worth the risk. He called me a coward but I am here and where is he now? All that he achieved was to get some innocent hostages shot. I can only say that it was not a building that I recognized. The painting is probably still there and mouldering away. I am long past caring. Why does it matter? Your story is still complete."

'Monsieur Laroque pointed out how much better a story it would be if they could recover the painting and return it to its rightful place in the gallery. He became quite persuasive, almost hectoring, on the subject. Was there nobody else, he asked, who could place the building?

'"You could try the Comte de Liverac," I said. "He has been writing a history of the Resistance."

'Uncle Jules said that the comte would not be of much help because the comte had been asking him for details of the incident. He sighed and then said, "If your story really demands that you can point to the building, you had better try to find Hélène Mercier, the girl who took command of the attack on the train. She was the other passenger in the van and she was in the front seat."'

Helen had been listening intently to Jeanne's story. 'And that,' she said, 'would have been your cue to pipe up? Yes?'

Jeanne smiled happily. 'Indeed yes! I was, of course, very surprised. "There is a Hélène Mercier staying in the hotel at this very moment," I said, "because I have twice given her a massage. She certainly noticed my souvenirs. She is an old lady." You do not mind, Hélène?'

'Being referred to as an old lady? Of course not, silly child. It is what I am and I could not be anything else if your story were true. You may be one yourself, some day. Go on.'

Jeanne dimpled with mischievous amusement. 'I explained how you were a very nice old lady, much too gentle ever to have killed Germans. I said that I could more easily imagine you knitting socks for them.'

'You didn't!'

'But of course not, not really. But between ourselves I find it difficult to imagine you doing these things. You are very gentle.'

'One becomes gentler, child, as one grows older. Sixty years ago, after my mother had been murdered and I was ... I was assaulted, I was quite capable of doing what you call "these things". There was a huge fury in me. Make me angry enough and I can do these things.' Her voice fell. 'In Ethiopia, I saw a soldier killing children with a bayonet. I pulled the pin out of a grenade, dropped it into his pocket and I walked away. I walked away rather quickly.'

Jeanne considered her in silence for a long moment, blew out a breath and then shrugged and resumed her story. 'I said that you spoke little but that your French is very good and I have heard you speaking English with other clients of the hotel; that you never referred to the war but that when you came to me for massage you noticed my souvenirs. You said nothing but you gave a small sound of surprise and recognition. So, I said, you might well be the same lady. Great-Uncle Jules said that he must hurry and pay a call on you, for old times' sake. That seemed to disturb Monsieur Laroque.'

'As I told you it would,' Helen said. 'That was the twitching of the fly. If Jules and I were to get together we could recover the painting and leave him out in the cold. But if it all came to him too easily, he would suspect just the sort of confidence trick that he is accustomed to putting across. How did he carry that one off?'

'He called for the bill, to give himself time to think. Then he said that he would be pleased to buy dinner for both of you, my great-uncle and yourself, but that he would prefer to speak first to you in isolation, as he had done with us, rather than have your recollections clouded by those of somebody else.'

'Very quick thinking,' Helen said, 'and almost convincing.'

'I thought so too, Hélène. Great-Uncle Jules said *"Eh bien!"* rather testily. He said that after sixty years he could wait a little longer, but he asked me to warn him if it seemed that you were about to go away again, because he would not want to miss the chance to talk over old times with one who had been such a good friend. Hélène, were you and Great-Uncle Jules lovers?'

Helen thought that that was a matter of definition. 'That, my girl,' she said, 'is none of your business. Go on with the story.'

Jeanne shrugged. 'Soon after that the bill

was laid on the table and we thanked him for the meal. That was all.'

'And quite enough to be going on with,' Helen said. 'I think ... I think that we have made enough leaps forward for the moment. Perhaps we should recoil in order to jump the further. And, again, he must not find it too easy. It is when the fly is moving away that the fish strikes. It is time for another visit to my grandson.'

'A moment, Hélène.' Jeanne darted out of the room and returned after half a minute with a large desk diary. 'I may come with you again? I have no appointments for the rest of the week that can not be moved, and I can pay my own fares.'

'There is still no need for that, my child. You cheered the boy up and that was well worth an extra fare by Cut Price Airlines.'

Fifteen

By phoning ahead, Helen contrived to have a hire car with automatic gears waiting for them, so their travelling was less fraught than on the previous trip. Jeanne, who had passed the flights silent and her knuckles showing white, began to relax. Helen, who had become accustomed to driving on the right, gritted her teeth and pointed the snub bonnet towards the M23.

'You will find it easier, now that we have a car with automatic gears,' Jeanne said carefully in English. She had been practising her English at intervals on the pretext of making the fullest use of Helen while she was available as a teacher. Helen suspected another reason for the sudden wish to become bilingual.

Helen slotted the car into a gap in the motorway traffic before feeling free to reply. 'I'm beginning to think that I have made a mistake,' she said. 'It might be convenient to have another driver who could manage manual gears on a right-hand-drive car. There may come a time when I need a driver for a certain car and the practice could have been useful.'

'You would trust me with David's very precious Jaguar?' Jeanne asked in a small voice.

'David might prefer not to, so we won't mention it. I may not have the option. If my plan works, I shall want to get the car out of France very quickly and without having to return to collect my own car. And I do not have another driver.'

'Great-Uncle Jules?'

'Your great-uncle has never driven a car with manual gears. I would drive the Jaguar myself and let you drive my car, but there may be questions that we can not easily answer, and a young and pretty girl would be more believable as the driver of a valuable sports car. Any official would be more likely to ask you for a date.'

'You would really consider me to be pretty?'

'That is not really for another woman to judge but, yes, I suppose that you could be said to come just within that category. And to save you from having to answer the question, again yes, David thinks you're pretty too.'

During the three days of their second visit to Bracken House, Helen booked and paid for, and Jeanne suffered, four driving lessons with a local instructor. These were carefully timed to fall between the hours for hospital visiting. After three days, Jeanne's driving and confidence were both greatly improved and her English had also taken a big step forward. David was much more comfortable and making short voyages with a zimmer frame. Helen was pleased but piqued to find that his pleasure at receiving a visit from his grandmother was eclipsed by his delight at the arrival of Jeanne. Helen relaxed with a book while the two chatted, each in the other's language. She and Jeanne filled the intervals between hospital visits and driving lessons with dog walks and repeated cleaning and prettying of David's cottage.

What was proving to be a halcyon respite for each of them ended on the Friday morning with an early phone call from Marcel. Monsieur Laroque had been telephoning to the hotel regularly in the hope of speaking with Madame Mercier. He had been informed that her room was still reserved and that her luggage remained, but that the hotel staff did not know when she would return. He was now demanding her home address, which the hotel was refusing to provide.

It was time to return to the other world. That afternoon, after protracted farewells that lasted until Helen had almost to prise the young couple apart, they set off for the Hotel Marmande. Marcel was no longer on duty by the time when Helen's car drew up at the door, but Helen let it be known that she would now accept phone calls.

Helen slept uneasily, half expecting the bedside phone to ring at any moment. But she woke, dressed and broke her fast without any word from Laroque. She took to her room and waited. The view from her window, over the hotel garden, some fields and a section of river, was pleasing, but she was in no mood for quiet contemplation. Had they left it too long and given him time to select another victim and begin the stalk?

The call that she was waiting for came as she was preparing for dinner. To her surprise, he was still using the name Laroque, but when she came to think about it, his previous presence in the hotel would have made a change of name dangerous for him.

'My name is Laroque,' he began. His voice was polite, deferential but confident. 'You won't remember the name if you ever knew it, but we shared a dinner table a week ago. I did not realize that I was dining with a heroine of the Resistance, or I would have been more attentive.'

'You are kind, Monsieur.'

'Perhaps you would allow me to remedy the omission?'

Helen pretended to pause for thought. She kept her voice cold, like royalty approached by a flea-bitten member of the lower orders. 'Tell me, Monsieur, were you the silver-haired gentleman in shorts? Or the balding man with glasses? Or—?'

His voice was smiling. 'Allow me to save you from having to rack your memory, Madame. I am in my thirties with dark hair and I was wearing a dark blazer and pale flannels.'

'With a cravat instead of a tie?'

'I am flattered that you should remember. I'm calling to ask whether you will allow me to pay my respects by offering you dinner at your hotel.'

'Tell me, Monsieur. How did you learn my name and that I had ever had a connection with the Resistance?'

'That is a story that I shall be happy to tell you over dinner.'

He was giving the fly a twitch. Helen let a little time slip away and infused some warmth into her voice. 'I suppose that, having already accepted a glass of wine from you, I must consider that we have been introduced. But we had better not delay for too long. I may not be able to prolong my stay.'

'You accept? But that is excellent. Tomorrow I have to go to Bordeaux, a matter of family business, but I could be back and at your hotel by the hour of dinner. Perhaps you would be so kind as to reserve a table?'

'I will certainly do that.'

'In case I am a little delayed, you could order the meal on both our behalves,' he suggested. 'I recall how sensibly chosen your own meal was. You have my complete trust.'

And that, she thought as she disconnected, was the eternal cry of the confidence trickster. *I trust you* was implicitly followed by *so you can trust me.*

Sixteen

Jeanne, as Helen was about to learn, was self-employed, paying a rental for the use of the massage parlour with secretarial services also provided. Thus, in theory, she could choose her own days and times of business. In accordance with the customs of a predominantly Catholic country, she reserved Sundays for herself and for the few clients who were prepared to pay well over the norm to have their pains eased on the afternoon of Jeanne's day of rest. That day, she had no such lucrative appointments in the diary.

Partly to clear her own mind and boost her morale, Helen wanted a discussion of the latest moves with Jeanne and Jules. For the three to be seen together in public would be to risk some word getting back to

Laroque, who might just possibly have some hotel servant on his payroll. Jeanne suggested that the vacant massage parlour might suit. The adjoining hairdressing salon and the room used by the manicurist would be deserted.

The trio met by arrangement. The window was firmly closed and the blinds were drawn against prying eyes. Jules and Helen took the two chairs while Jeanne declared herself perfectly comfortable, perched on the lowered massage table.

'I have had a call from the comte,' Helen said. 'Laroque visited him by appointment on Thursday. Laroque pretended to be a fellow writer, embarking on a biography of Hélène Mercier, seeking additional material and also making sure that the two books do not cover the same material.'

'Ingenious,' said Jules. 'But I would have enjoyed hearing the two, each pretending to be an author.'

'I don't know about Laroque, but Gaspard must have carried conviction or Laroque would not have made contact with me. A biography of me, indeed! No doubt with a picture on the dust jacket of some skinny model with a tommy gun, a grenade and a railway engine in the background. Some day I may be in a position to ask him for sight of the typescript. I don't know where these people get their ideas about me.'

'Legends grow like weeds,' Jules said, 'but there is some truth in this one.'

'Much beating of the water with a stick.'

'The incident of the train...'

'As I remember it,' said Helen, 'when poor Henri was taken, the men were saying "That's it, then" and I only said that we still had his plan and why didn't we go ahead with it? Everybody said "Yes" and waited for me to cry *"En avant!"* It all grew from there.'

'And the German you killed? Nobody says it aloud,' Jules said. 'Everybody knows but such things are not spoken of. There might still be repercussions. The man may have left a wife and children, and you were not acting even on the informal authority of the Resistance. But that's all water under the bridge now.'

'I sincerely hope so,' Helen said. 'Let's

leave it there to float out to sea. What I want to discuss is the line to take when I meet Laroque. What he wants is to get from each of us our piece of the information, but I think that we should insist on meeting him together. It would be too blatant to demand a bribe, but I was thinking of insisting on a contribution to some charity. I would have enjoyed inventing a charity called something like Restitution for Victims of Fraud, but that would be too close to home and he would certainly see through it. I am not intending to profit from this; I shall be happy if we can recover the car and precisely the sum that he stole from my grandson but, once again, mention of that precise sum might start him thinking.' She looked at Jules consideringly.

'I need no reward,' said Jules with dignity. 'The affair remains interesting and I have already dined well on it.'

'I already have a reward,' Jeanne said. She was prone to blushing and she was blushing now. Her elders regarded her with amused tolerance. 'Something more precious than money,' she said defiantly. She was looking at the ceiling. 'Last night I phoned David in the hospital to tell him that you had heard from Laroque, or Lemaître as he knows him. We talked for hours; the hotel can well afford the cost of the call. You do not mind?' she asked Helen anxiously. 'He is mending well and he sent you his love.'

'The hotel might have something to say about it,' Helen said, 'but I have no objection. You would certainly be a more suitable companion for him than those few of his lady friends that he has allowed me to meet in the past, but that is entirely a matter for the pair of you.' She was careful to let no sign show of the glow of pleasure that was warming her inner self. She had become very attached to Jeanne and in her love for David she had worried how he would manage alone when her time was up. In a whimsical moment she had thought that she would not have hesitated to kidnap Jeanne and present her to David, wrapped up in a pink ribbon on a black velvet cushion, if that would have given him pleasure. 'Now, Jeanne,' she said, 'let us move on. We must be ready for every turn that our discussion with him may take. Your great-uncle and I will be ourselves. You will be Monsieur Laroque. You wish to gain from us the whereabouts of the painting and you wish to pay as little as possible for the information. We are dining together, you and I. Begin!'

The telephone interrupted a mock argument in which Jeanne, in the guise of Monsieur Laroque, was trying with great fluency to persuade her great-uncle into divulging the precise whereabouts of the hiding place in the structure of the unidentified building, and Jules was protesting that it would be impossible to transmit such information precisely and that he would have to be taken to the site in order to refresh his memory.

Jeanne picked up the phone. 'Yes? Yes, she is with me now but her treatment is almost finished. I come. You have a visitor,' she told Helen. 'A lady. She says that you would not know her name but she has information of importance. I will go?'

'Please do,' said Helen. 'If it concerns this matter, I would wish you both to know. If she is only another person with an axe to grind, I will send her about her business and you can watch and learn how the hardened expert gets rid of an unwanted visitor.'

Jeanne grinned and hurried out.

'You think,' said Jules, 'that Jeanne and your grandson...?'

Helen shrugged. 'Did you ever see two people go to mush at the sight of each other?'

'Now and again. Is that how it was? It could, I think, have been much worse. I have not met your David but I sense that Jeanne has lost her heart to him.'

'That is certainly true. David is a good boy and a clever engineer.' She paused for a moment. There were certain criteria by which the French tended to judge a forthcoming marriage. 'He has property and he will always be a good earner, but he is not wise in the ways of the world and, when it comes to women, he is a child. Your Jeanne could have been made for him. I would have been prepared to give the affair a little push, but it is quite unnecessary. I am sorry about Marcel.'

It was Jules's turn to shrug. 'That is your

tender heart speaking. He will get over it, probably. He lacks strength of character, that one. He was never worthy of Jeanne. It is not always easy for a girl from a good background with expectations to meet suitable young men. But she never dreamed of Marcel as she does of David. When the flame of physical desire begins to cool, there will still—'

He was interrupted by the reappearance of Jeanne with another woman in tow. Helen guessed the woman's age as late twenties, but within a few seconds realized that she was younger. She was small and slender so that her bones seemed fragile. She wore a trouser suit with a long-sleeved jacket, both dated and showing signs of wear. Her black hair had not had expert attention for a long time. She was clearly in an advanced state of agitation, continuously tucking her lank hair behind her ears. 'You are Hélène Mercier?'

'I am,' said Helen. 'And you are...?'

The question seemed to add to the young woman's stress. 'My name does not matter, not ever or to anybody. Yesterday, I heard an account of your services to the Resistance and I salute you, Madame. I envy you the chance you had to be of such service. *He* was laughing at it and then *he* said something...' She choked into silence.

'Who?' Helen asked gently. 'And said what? You came here to tell me something.'

The visitor took several deep breaths. Then it came with a rush. 'What he said told me that he intends to dupe you as he has so many others. I could not let that happen, not to one of your courage who had served France so well. So I came to warn you. Do not trust the man you are to dine with this evening. Please believe me. I am taking a terrible risk just coming here.'

'This is very interesting,' said Helen. 'But why did you come? Why not telephone?'

The woman produced a twisted smile. '*He* will not have a telephone installed. It would make him easier to trace, you see. *He* carries a mobile phone everywhere. And *he* never leaves me any money, none at all. Also, you would not have believed a voice on the phone. But he left the garage unlocked to-day and his other car had some petrol in the tank, so I was able to come and show you.'

With a quick shake of the head, she had refused the chair that Jules had offered. There were other clues in her posture that Helen had noticed without understanding, but the masseuse was more practised at reading body language. She leaned forward suddenly and pushed up the other woman's sleeve. The woman jumped back and brushed down her sleeve while her face turned scarlet. She lowered her head – to hide tears, Helen thought. Helen was puzzled. The glimpse of the other woman's arm had been too brief for her to see any detail, but if there were needle-marks she had not seen them. Jeanne, grim-faced, stooped and lifted one cuff of the woman's trousers. Then Helen saw them. Rope marks, unmistakably imprinted.

'That is what you were going to show me?'

She nodded and then pushed back her hair again.

Jules got up and gently steered the woman into his chair. She submitted, child-like, but she looked at Helen.

'If he did that to you,' Helen said, 'it's no wonder that you use a special tone of voice when you say *he* or *him*.'

'It doesn't matter,' the woman said, her voice barely above a whisper. '*I* don't matter. It has nothing to do with this.'

'But you must leave him,' Jeanne said.

'There is nowhere that I can go. I have no family, no friends.' She sighed. Suddenly the need to speak overcame shyness and shame and she began to gabble. 'It's an old story with new twists. I came to him as his secretary four or five – no, six – years ago, when I was seventeen. He can show great charm when he wishes. I was romantic and stupid. He very soon made me his mistress. We were to be married, he said. Instead, I realized that he was making me his toy. He is a sadist. He enjoys ... not just giving pain, but control, power, total power.' She pushed up her sleeve and this time Helen saw the rope marks. 'It gives him so much pleasure to control, to hurt. In the beginning, when I still adored him, I was almost glad. To give him pleasure I would suffer the humiliations, the pain, the bonds. Perhaps that was what they mean by "the Stockholm syndrome". If he had loved me I would have accepted him as he was, but as time went by he got worse and I realized that to him I was only a body to be abused, to gratify him by screaming aloud.'

'How could you possibly stay with him?' Jeanne whispered.

'There was no clear-cut moment at which a line was crossed. At first, as I told you, I was willing. It's not all bad, you know. To be the totally passive partner with no decisions to make, that is peaceful; and when one has no choice there is no sense of guilt.

'For as long as I showed fear and cringed from pain, he was pleased with me. I became hardened to it so I pretended, but he saw through me and became worse, much worse. Soon, I had a nervous break-down and he had me declared mentally handicapped. I did not resist. I thought that it might buy me a little peace in some institution. I was never so deluded. Later, when it became too much and I ran away, he had me returned to his care. Some care! I am his toy. He delights in his cruelty and I can do nothing but endure and wait for the release of death.' She fell silent, standing with her head lowered, but in the silence they could a muffled sob.

Helen had encountered abuse in its various forms and had known that she could only report; action in individual cases had been beyond her scope. But this was very bad. 'You must run away,' she said.

The young woman raised her head and pushed back her hair. Her face was disfigured by torment and tears. 'I'm sorry,' she said. Her voice was shaking. She wrung her hands together. 'I only came to warn you. I've no right to burden you with troubles I brought on myself with my own stupidity. I would run away again if I could, but I have nowhere to go. If I ran away now, penniless and friendless, I might fall into worse hands. That first time, I ran to the police, but he swore that I was paranoid and that he had restrained me for my own safety. He had witnesses, one of them a doctor who loves to join in the fun. And me, I have nothing. Nothing and nobody. And no way out. Look.' She pulled up one leg of her trouser suit and they saw the weals, some old and some very fresh. 'He almost never marks me where I could not have managed to mark myself, and when he goes further than that he keeps me shut up until the marks have healed. Often when he goes out he leaves me chained or tied. It excites him to think of me waiting there, as helpless as a parcel.'

There was silence in the room except for the thin sound that Helen recognized as half-controlled sobs.

'He has not addicted you to any drugs?' Jules asked.

The woman shook her head. 'No, thank God. He had made me sniff drugs sometimes, but never the needle. He is too careful. You see, the marks might show. And now I must get back. If he came home early and caught me, he would think of something worse than ever. One day he will kill me and it will all be over.'

'Be brave for a little longer,' Jules said. 'I think that the end may be nearer than you think. Just endure and say nothing to him.'

She nodded. 'You only tell me to do what I do always.' Jeanne led her out.

'Were you thinking of demanding some extra money from Laroque, so that she would not have to face the world penniless?' Helen asked Jules.

He shook his head. 'Laroque would only swear that she had stolen it from him. No. This is not one of those problems that will run away if you throw money at it. You heard her say that she had been a secretary. The business was about to engage another clerk. There is a tiny flat there that Jeanne once occupied before there was room for her in the staff quarters of the hotel. There are never less than four or five men within call of that flat.' He sighed heavily. 'Life has given me so much, it is time that I gave something back to somebody less fortunate than I.'

'And it is not possible that this is another of his tricks?'

Jules made a face. 'I do not think that any-one is such an actress, nor would she hurt herself so. But if it is a trick and we do not give her money, the trick has failed.'

'You are right,' Helen said. 'But I am sure that she is real. At least we now know why he chooses to live isolated in the country. What you suggest will answer very well.'

Seventeen

Helen took some care with her toilet the following evening. It seemed vital that she present the right picture. Rather than the sweet-little-old-lady image that she had used so often and so effectively, she was aiming more towards the grande dame who would stand no nonsense from tradesmen and, more crucially, would consider any sums of money less than the price of a new car to be beneath her notice. Fortunately this was much the impression that, out of surprise and caution, her conduct when they had met earlier across the dinner table must have conveyed. She had only to build on his recollection of that occasion.

Laroque had phoned from his car to warn her of his probable time of arrival, so when the desk phoned her room to advise her that her visitor had arrived and was waiting in the lounge, she was ready, in a dress that was both tasteful and obviously expensive, and a small but discreetly valuable selection of jewellery. She was conscious of a faint fluttering in her vitals and an uncertainty in her knees as she walked through to the foyer, but the sensation of imminent drama was an old friend, no more than nature's way of warning her to be ready with the required supply of adrenaline. Laroque must have been similarly affected, but his manner conveyed no more than respectful interest and a quiet confidence befitting a respectable man of the world.

Laroque came out to meet her in the hall. He was smart in a good suit, a new shirt and a modest tie that looked as though it belonged to some club or regiment, although if this were the case, it was not one that Helen had ever encountered. He seemed freshly shaved; Helen guessed that either he had an electric shaver in his car or the hotel had facilities in the Gents. He was certainly freshly washed and his nails had been filed.

He had had more sense than to bring a corsage, which would have struck the wrong note by being more suited to a romantic date. Instead, he treated her to the *baise-main*, kissing air above her hands, and led her back into the lounge, enquiring what she would take as an apéritif. His manners were perfect, an essential for any successful confidence trickster. He gave an excellent impression of a cultured admirer who wanted no more than to honour a national heroine. After a few minutes of exposure to so much carefully cultivated courtesy, she had to remind herself that this was the man who had robbed her grandson, indirectly caused David's nearly fatal accident, committed an outrage on her photograph and made a slave of a previously innocent young woman.

As Jules and Jeanne had reported, he conversed easily during the meal about current topics, moving quickly away from Helen's wartime experiences to a general chat about such diverse subjects as the farming crisis, an impending railway strike, the prospects of the wine industry and the latest government scandal. He recounted some of the latest jokes. She accepted his choice of wines and found it to be excellent. He was both amusing and well informed; if she had not known him for a rogue, she just might have accepted him at face value, and she made up her mind to reassure David that there was no shame in having been taken in by such an expert. Allowing her manner to thaw slightly, she wondered in what school he had obtained his education in fraud.

When they had arrived at the dessert course, he led the conversation back to Helen's youthful adventures. 'The story of the railway train still fascinates me,' he said. 'It was a noble attempt to prevent the theft of some of our national treasures. Have you any idea how much of it was ever recovered?'

Helen, who had been out of France for nearly sixty years, had not the faintest idea, but it seemed better to make a guess. 'When last I heard,' she said, 'less than half, but it was the more valuable half. That is excluding the Fragonard painting, of course.' She let a faint, knowing smile show. 'That would be of very great value.'

'They tell me that the Germans did not get away with it.'

'Oh? And what else, may I ask, do they tell you?'

He spoke slowly, choosing his words with care. 'They say that a small party escaped with it and that it still lies hidden where they put it. And I am told that the driver of the van was the only one who knew the precise hiding place and he was killed soon afterwards. The painting has never surfaced again.'

She nodded. 'I believe that to be so.' In fact, she knew it to be so, except that the painting, according to an underworld contact, was believed to have been sold by a senior member of the Nazi party and had vanished into the collection of an Argentinean cattle baron. She had tried to follow up the story years before, but had met with a stone wall.

'I am told that you were one of that party.' He paused and looked at her with innocent eyes. 'Do you think that the painting may perhaps have been recovered and sold to some billionaire American collector? Or have you never felt an urge to attempt a recovery?'

Though the suggestion was oblique, it was open to her to treat it as an insult or as a provocation. But he was too close to the truth. Instead, she pretended to consider it calmly. 'I think that very unlikely,' she said. 'No one person knows where it lies hidden. And no, I am not inclined to aid its recovery.' She leaned forward. He leaned towards her until their heads were secretively close. He expected a revelation and he was not disappointed. The story had been created by Helen and polished by Jeanne and Jules until it glowed with seductive highlights.

'I will tell you something, Monsieur, which is not generally known. That painting once belonged to my family, which is why its early history is largely unrecorded. But my father had sustained losses on the *Bourse*. This was in the 'thirties. He was forced to sell many of the family assets. That one painting alone would have cleared all his debts. But a man came, from a ministry or perhaps from the gallery, I forget, if I ever knew – for I was hardly out of the cradle. He convinced my father that the painting was the work of a lesser man, a mere copyist of Fragonard's work. He knew the life histories of Fragonard and the copyist and he spoke with conviction about craquelure and brush-strokes and the chemistry of oil paints. The painting was sold for a fraction of its value. Then, of course, there was a sudden fanfare and the ministry was credited with the discovery of a master-piece.

'My father, of course, tried to make a fuss, but he had no witnesses and nothing in writing. The ministry was adamant that no such discussion had taken place, that the painting had been purchased from an independent dealer and that the man had not had any official standing. Later, he learned that this was untrue. He went to see the man, who laughed in his face.

'Well, Monsieur Laroque, I care deeply about national treasures. Any other treasure I will spill my own blood to restore to the nation, but that one can stay where it is until it moulders.'

She sat back. Had she, she wondered, pushed it too far? She had known for years how to twitch a fly, as she had explained to Jeanne, so that a trout could not resist lunging for it. She had used the same technique to obtain an interview with a Beirut terrorist leader and with his hostage. She knew suddenly that she was about to get a rise. By the set of his mouth and a tiny shift around his eyes, she knew that he was ready to snatch at the bait. She sipped her wine and looked around the room as if admiring the mirrored opulence of the décor and the dresses of the other women. She could feel him thinking. If only she could feel his thoughts; but, alas, that degree of rapport between angler and fish was denied her.

'I sympathize,' he said suddenly. 'Such a history would sicken me. But it is not my history. I have no distaste for the painting. I would like to see it restored. No, hear me out,' he added as she raised her nose and flared her nostrils in an attitude copied from a great lady whom she had once interviewed about a disastrous marriage. 'I would not suggest that you make the nation a present of it – your family has already been too generous in that respect. Nor would I expect you to lower yourself to haggling over a reward for its return. But I would be delighted to negotiate its return and to collect a very substantial reward on your behalf. If, as you say, your father was unfortunate with his investments, a fresh injection of finance surely could not come amiss.'

She waited, pretending deep thought. 'I would not look for anything for myself,' she said at last. 'My late husband had his faults but he was a good provider. A friend is planning a project, a refuge for battered wives.' She was holding his eyes. Had she strayed too close to a nerve? But no. He was hanging on her words. 'I have been helping to raise money. It is a project very dear to me. You see, a lady, a friend of mine since our schooldays, recently took her own life. It turned out that her husband, such a respectable man, had been beating her regularly. For a substantial contribution to that charity, I might be prepared to help.'

'You could certainly trust me to get the reward to you,' he said. She could see his elation, hear it in his voice, even smell it.

'I don't think so,' she said. 'Like my father, God rest him, I have trusted too many people in my life. What I want is a contribution in cash – not a cheque but cash – and I'll give you a receipt that you can use for tax purposes.'

'Why not a cheque?' he asked sharply.

'Because I must get home very shortly and I can not wait around for cheques to clear. You must have seen how reluctant French banks have become to release money to anyone other than a local account-holder. Also because, even if the bank has assured the recipient that there are funds to cover it, a cheque may still bounce, even weeks later. Did you know that, Monsieur Laroque?'

He shook his head, although she thought that he was perfectly aware of the intricacies of stolen identity. She thought that he was trying to decide whether to be alarmed or respectful at her knowledge. The fact of her suspicions seemed only to induce a sense of fellow feeling. 'How much did you have in mind?' he asked her.

They settled down to negotiate. Helen was greatly helped by knowing exactly the figure below which she was not going to budge – the amount stolen from David, rounded up to avoid a suspicious coincidence and to allow for her considerable expenditure. Each might be aiming to deceive, but when it came to the crunch they were both born hagglers. Indeed, she soon came to realize that each was enjoying the argument for its own sake, irrespective of the financial outcome. She expressed contempt for the figure that he first offered; he pretended outrage at her first suggestion. Two Grand Marniers apiece later, they settled precisely on her intended figure. 'And you may leave me to settle with Jules Petiot,' she said.

She saw him twitch. 'How did you know?'

She laughed at him. 'I remember who the third man was, the one who went into the building. You will need him. I have no idea what happened inside. You are in touch with him? He is still alive?'

'I had forgotten that part of the story,' he

admitted. 'Yes, I have spoken with him. If he is shown the building, he can do the rest. If you settle with him, we have a deal. When can we bring it to a conclusion?'

'The sooner the better. The building is now occupied, I think by some sort of a religious college where occasional courses are held. There are caretakers, so a visit by night will be necessary. I would suggest tonight, except that I do not think that you could get such a sum in cash at this time of night.'

'Tomorrow night, then? I could have the money by then.'

'Tomorrow night. You speak to Monsieur Petiot. Phone me if he can not be available. If I do not hear from you, we will meet at midnight precisely.'

While they spoke, settling details, she could sense his attitude shifting from caution to excitement. Already the painting was almost within his grasp, too close to allow details to frighten him off. The trout had grabbed the fly. The customary percentage reward alone would far more than cover the promised payment. But if he could tout it around the super-rich of the world, it would set him up for life. His enjoyment was only a little marred by the emergence of the charming old lady as a tough negotiator who had no intention of parting with any information until she could see hard cash and who, if dissatisfied, had expressed herself quite prepared to deal direct with Jules Petiot and leave him out in the cold. There were not so many Petiots in the telephone directory, she said. She had considered looking for her old friend. Jules had said he was thinking of paying a call on her. He would have to move quickly.

Jeanne had promised to wait for a phone call, but she must have been lurking just beyond the staff doorway near Helen's room. Helen had entered her room and was removing her few jewels when there came a soft rap on the door.

'All is arranged, Hélène?'

'Indeed yes.' Helen explained the agreements that she had reached with Laroque and her plans for the next night. 'Seat yourself. You can be free for a few days?' she asked anxiously. A vital part of her planning depended on having a second driver, and she would prefer to get out of France quickly.

Jeanne seemed nervous, which was unlike her. 'I can be free. This is a quiet time of year. But, Hélène...'

'Yes? Speak, child,' Helen said kindly.

'Madame ... I mean Hélène. I spoke to David again last night, another long call. He sends his love and the doctors are very pleased with him.' There was a pause and when she spoke again it was in a very quiet tone. 'If I come with you, I think that I shall not be coming back to France. I told him that he should be the one to speak to you and to my family, but he said that you had already guessed and that my French is better than his. You do not mind?' Surely there was a blush beneath the careful make-up?

'Of course I don't mind,' Helen said warmly. 'I think that you are just what David needs most. I will not pry into your plans, but you will be welcome to stay with me until you are both ready. But what about

Marcel? Will he be angry enough to betray us?'

Jeanne laughed. 'Marcel has other strings to his bow. I have already explained to him, but he did not seem unhappy. I think perhaps that he was relieved. And I have left a letter with him to give to the hotel if I do not return, terminating my tenancy and suggesting that my clients be referred to Janine. My luggage is packed. Great-Uncle Jules wished me happy. He will send on the rest of my things. He said that any grandson of yours would be a worthy husband.'

'That was a very kind thing to say.' Helen got up and gave the girl a hug. 'Husband, though? Have things progressed so far?'

Jeanne produced a mischievous smile. 'Hélène ... or should I say Maman? ... I would not live with him on any other terms. Already we began to plan our family. We wish for two boys and a girl.'

Helen studied the girl. So young, so almost innocent ... She decided that there was a great deal of accumulated wisdom that she could pass on to Jeanne, comprising all the things that she wished that somebody had told her when she was young. Perhaps if her mother had survived, Helen might not have been left to puzzle out some of life's lessons for herself. 'You may call me Maman later,' she said. 'That is one of several things that should wait until after you are married. We shall have to have a long talk very soon. But for now we must phone your great-uncle. I shall tell him how happy I am but also how we shall progress tomorrow.'

'But you must also phone David and tell him that you are pleased.'

Jeanne was insistent, but Helen, knowing hospital routine, thought that David would already have been settled to sleep. 'In the morning, child,' she said. 'I promise.'

Eighteen

Helen rested for much of the day. She had advised Jeanne to do the same, although the young were more able to manage with minimal sleep. Win or lose, there would be an exhausting time ahead, during which she might need all her wits and her available strength. The day dragged. Sleep evaded her except for a brief period after lunch, but at least she was still physically fresh when the time had come to prepare. Dark, warm clothing was already laid out. The rest was carefully packed.

Helen and Laroque had arranged to meet at a crossroads, selected by Helen, so that they would arrive at the building from a direction that would not be too informative to Laroque. Her account at the hotel had been settled and there was luggage for two in the boot of her car. She had never been so prone to nerves in the old days, but she was out of practice and, during her career, she had not had a personal stake in the outcome. She drove with butterflies in her stomach and a feeling that her bowels might loosen. She was first at the rendezvous and pulled off on to an area of dry grass.

The next steps had been carefully scripted. Laroque arrived soon after her, but she suspected that he had remained out of sight to observe her arrival from a distance. In his shoes she would have done the same, in case the whole operation was aimed at a hijack of the money. She was pleased to note that, as if he wanted to further her plans, Laroque was wearing one of his smart suits. If he had come in dungarees, part of her grand design would have had to be exchanged for Plan B. Jules turned up a few minutes later, precisely on the midnight hour.

Laroque watched without any show of impatience as the two made a carefully rehearsed show of greeting each other apparently after a gap of many years. It had been agreed that Jules would sit in his car but in plain view while Helen entered Laroque's Audi to conduct their business. He had the money, a substantial slab of new hundred-Euro notes, in an attaché case that he held firmly on his knee. He allowed Helen to slip out several notes chosen at random. The numbers all differed. She had taken the precaution of drawing several similar notes fresh from the bank that morning and had brought them carefully sealed in a polythene envelope. The feel and smell are more likely to betray the forgery than defects in the printing, but these seemed identical. She decided that the money was genuine because Laroque would not have risked queering the whole deal to save his initial stake.

At her insistence, the case remained on the passenger seat in Laroque's Audi. Inconspicuously, she passed a hand through the rear footwells and checked there was not enough space under her seat for a similar case. If he could still substitute attaché cases while driving the car and under the eye of Jules in the car behind, he was more of a magician than she judged him to be.

Helen returned to her own car and led the

way. She made a show of hesitating at junctions and brought them by a circuitous route. This, she had explained, would be because she would be following from memory a route over which she had been driven after the attack on the train; in fact, her real reason was that the more direct route would have entailed passing a large signboard that would have presented Laroque with information that she preferred him to be without. She had to hope that he had never driven past her intended destination. The contingency had seemed unlikely when she made her plans, but now she was becoming uncomfortably aware that a man who lived in the same general area might well have found that road to be a convenient short cut. Could fate have been so cruel? But it was a very minor road, not the best route from anywhere to anywhere else and only serving a few farms and the one large building. She watched the Audi's lights in the mirror and was heartened to see a changed driving style as they left one road for another of even less importance. There were several turnings where the road margins were out of sight until the last moment. Laroque was hesitant, dropping back as they approached instead of meeting the bend with the confidence of familiarity.

Forty minutes later, they parked on rough grass near the gates of the large building and left the cars, walking softly along the mown verge beside the drive under a three-quarter moon. There was no sign that Laroque had ever been there before. Helen felt the chill of the night-time dew through the thin leather of her shoes, and she was glad of the warmth of her tweed coat. For once, Helen was nervous. If Laroque had sensed it he would have put it down to the night and the mission, but Helen was only anxious for the artistic integrity of her plan. No doubt Laroque considered his confidence tricks to be artistically perfect. Helen intended her revenge to be poetic, beautiful and ruthless, but Laroque's suspicions might germinate again, in which case she was quite prepared to fell him with the hammer that she had borrowed from Jules and was hiding beneath her coat. Jules, she knew, was similarly equipped, but with a tyre lever in his bag of tools. It was designed for dealing with tractor tyres and it was heavy. Despite his fancy for sadism, Laroque, she kept telling herself, was not a man of action. Even two pensioners, equipped with blunt instruments, could expect to deal with him. He might well intend to use some form of intimidation to save or recover the money, but not until they had the painting.

She brought them to the window that she had selected. 'This is truly the place,' Jules said softly. 'Until this moment I was uncertain, but this is the very window by which we entered. And I have done this once already.' He took out a small tool from his bag and forced it into the join of the casement window. With no more than a sharp click and a rattle, the latch yielded and the window was half opened. Jules reached in with a gloved hand and unbolted the other half. Then, following Helen's plan to the letter, he looked into the cellar by torchlight and made a small sound of disgust. He removed his jacket and began to unbutton his shirt.

'What are you doing?' Laroque demanded, urgently but in a murmur.

'This room has been used as a cellar,' Jules whispered. 'There is sawdust and bits of leaf and bark everywhere. Where the painting is hidden, there is the dust and cobwebs of sixty years or more. At this time of night, the motorcycle police are at their most suspicious and cars are often stopped. We may have to explain ourselves before this night is over. You can please yourself, but you will be the one carrying the painting. If I look respectable I shall be believed, even at my age, when I explain that I am on my way home from a romantic rendezvous. I'm taking my suit off for the moment.'

Laroque hesitated, suspicious but half-sold by the reminder that he would be carrying the painting.

'Go ahead,' Helen whispered. 'At my age, I've seen it all before.'

Her comment soothed Laroque immediately. He gave a small snort of amusement but he said, 'That seems sensible.' In a minute, he was down to his socks, shoes and underpants, and folding his clothes together on the grass.

Jules, similarly disrobed, showed a layer of fat appropriate to his age, but he was heavily muscled. He picked up his toolbag. 'Hop down and take this from me,' he said.

Immediately, Laroque's suspicions flared again. 'You go first. I'll hand it down to you.'

Jules nodded, smiled and moved suddenly forward. Jules was much the heavier of the two. He gave Laroque a barge that tumbled him over the sill. They heard the man fall heavily down into the basement. The need for silence was so deeply instilled that he gave no more than a gasp.

Laroque scrambled to his feet. His face, instantly transformed, glared up at them from an arm's length below their level. He wasted no time on questions or protests but made a jump, grabbed the sill and began to haul himself up, preparatory to scrambling out. As his face came into the moonlight, Helen saw how rage and suspicion had taken over from greed, but he was looking at Jules, not at her. She decided that he was so accustomed to defrauding gentle old ladies that the idea of retaliation from one of their number never crossed his mind.

Helen had already unclipped the hammer from the belt of her dress and decided which of his fingers would be most likely to be crushed if the window had been caught by a gust of wind. There was just enough breeze to make such a scenario credible.

Even knowing him for what he was, she had to steel herself. During her career, much of which had been spent on the fringes of the world's worst violence, she had on occasions had to injure or kill. She had gone on firearms courses and had fired shots in anger. But most of those incidents had been in self-defence or in circumstances so terrible that she had been driven by an awful fury. This, however, was a matter of cold revenge and she had not realized how the inhibitions of so many years of civilization would check her hand.

Laroque had raised himself until his centre of gravity was at the level of the sill. They locked eyes and she saw in his eyes some of the evil that his slave must have seen only too often. She pictured the girl's terror and remembered her grandson's daaged body, and she raised the hammer.

His face changed. He made a frantic effort to roll over the sill before she could strike but his fingers were still on the lower rail of the window frame. He ducked his head, as he thought, away from her swing. But she nerved herself and brought the hammer down with all her strength on the first and second fingers of his right hand. In the sound of the blow she was sure that she heard bone snap.

Breaking the long near-silence with a howl of agony, Laroque fell back.

Jules was already struggling into his trousers. Helen rolled up Laroque's clothes into a bundle, took it under her arm and set off towards the cars. Jules caught her up before she reached the gates. They hurried in silence. There had already been sufficient noise. Lights were coming on behind them.

'He won't be able to climb out, with at least one broken finger and probably two, will he?' Helen asked as soon as they were well out of earshot from the building.

'If he does, he is Superman. You surprised me. I had not known that you were still so ruthless.'

'Be thankful that you have never seen me truly angry.'

Jeanne, who had travelled curled up under a rug on the back seat of Jules's car, was waiting for them. 'It went well?' she asked.

'To perfection.'

Laroque's car keys were on a ring with other keys in his pocket. Helen unrolled his clothes, found the keys and collected the attaché case. If, despite her reasoning, the money turned out to be counterfeit, she would come back and do something even more terrible to Laroque. Just to make life difficult for him, she was tempted to lock his car with his clothes inside, abstract his house keys and throw the car key into the bushes, but after his arrest any such detail might have put a flaw in the carefully contrived picture. She left the keys dangling from the ignition.

'Next, his house,' she said. 'And we must hurry. The police will already have been alerted.' Her car led the way again. This time, Jeanne sat beside her. After a few yards they passed the large signboard. It read: *Convent of the Sacred Heart.*

Nineteen

Laroque's house sat dark and quiet under the moonlight. In the open countryside it seemed to lurk in the square of trees and undergrowth like a predator waiting to pounce. Rather than risk their cars being seen nearby, perhaps bolstering some story of Laroque's, they parked again in the track through the wood and the three of them hurried the length of the field. Of one thing they could be sure: the occupier was not at home. They crunched over the gravel. No sensor lights came on, but they could hear a warning electronic squeal from inside the house.

The garage door proved to be a stouter defence than Jules had expected. It took him several minutes and some loud bangs before the first half could be opened, and

Helen gave thanks for the lack of close neighbours. The alarms would certainly not be linked to the police station; Laroque was as capable as she was of envisaging the police, summoned by an electronic fault or the passing of some animal, arriving and feeling obliged to enter the house. The garage was well equipped, though rather barren by David's standards. The E-type Jaguar was still where she had last seen it – waiting perhaps for a buyer or for a change of registration, or possibly for Laroque to tire of his new trophy. She pulled off the dust sheet and threw it aside. The original registration numbers were still displayed. Helen had been carrying David's spare key since her first visit. She moved towards the car and then hesitated.

The sound of the alarm had cut off. Faintly, she could hear a voice calling from inside the house. The voice was definitely calling for help. She thought that she could make out the words, *'M'aidez. M'aidez.'*

Helen very much wanted to be well away before there was any chance of the police following up any fairy tale told by Laroque;

but they could hardly leave his slave to his tender mercies if he managed to return home, or to starve if he remained in custody. She led her small party to the front door. The squeal of the alarm started again. Jules studied the lock and then went to work with a tool from his bag. This door was easier. It swung open.

Helen switched on lights. 'Wait here, child,' she told Jeanne. 'If you hear a car coming or see its lamps, kill the lights.' There was a fuse box in a small cupboard beside the door and she identified the main switch for Jeanne.

Jules was on her heels as she hurried from room to room, searching for the source of the cries. The house was luxuriously furnished, though without any pretence of good taste. The third room that they visited was more Spartan and in it, at the foot of a large metal-framed bed, they found the young woman who had come to the hotel. She was lying face down on the floor, nude but for a thong. Her wrists and ankles were chained together. Her shoulders and buttocks were striped with lash-marks and goose-pimpled by the cold, and when she turned her head, her face was tear-streaked. 'Thank God!' she said. 'Thank God!'

The shackles had the most secure locks that they had so far encountered. 'Where does he keep the key?' Helen asked.

'On his ring in his pocket.'

Again Helen regretted leaving Laroque's keys in his car. Verisimilitude might be all very well but practicality came first.

'I think that I saw a bolt cutter in the garage,' Jules said. 'I will fetch it.'

'Don't leave me here,' the young woman croaked. She was weeping with fear. 'If he gets angry, God knows what he'll do to me. I couldn't have prevented you, but that never stopped him yet. He blames me if a passing bird shits on him.'

Helen knelt down beside the girl. 'We'll get you out of here,' she said, 'even if we have to carry you like that. He will never lay a finger on you again, I promise you. Why did he leave you chained? Did he know you had been to see us?'

'It was just a whim of his,' she said. 'It excited him to think of me lying helpless until he decided to come back from cheating you.' Tears were still streaming across her cheeks, but otherwise she had control of herself. 'When I heard the alarm, I knew that strangers had come, and something told me that it had to be you. And that meant that I had to get away because, as I said, if he came home and found that his house had been entered, he would be furious; and when he loses his temper he is the devil incarnate. He can think of nothing but being revenged on the world.' She drew a shuddering breath. 'His mind turns first to me and he can think of tortures that you could never imagine. It can be very bad.'

'I know. I can see the marks.'

She gave a bitter imitation of a laugh. 'There's worse than that. Much worse. Just to start with, he has an electric cattle prod.'

'Be patient,' Helen said after a pause. 'Arrangements have been made. A job and your own small flat and men nearby who would come if you called—'

'Dear God, if only that could be true it would be beyond—'

At that moment, the lights went out. In

the darkness, she heard the other woman make a sound of fear.

'It's probably nothing,' Helen said, 'but stay very quiet.' She got up and felt her way into the hall. The front door was tight shut.

'I saw the lights of a car,' Jeanne whispered. 'I think it's coming here.' They waited. Helen found that her mouth was dry. They were no longer acting out a script that she had drafted but following random events outside her control, forced to react in ways that she could not predict. She had left the hammer in her car. A vehicle's lights dragged across the front of the house and stopped. The lights died but the car sat quiet for a full minute. Then they heard the car's door open and close. Footsteps dragged nearer. They seemed to be carrying the weight of the world. A key was fumbled into the lock and the door opened. There came the sound of breathing, laboured and pained.

'Lights,' Helen said. There was a loud gasp from the direction of the door.

The lights flared on. Laroque stood in the doorway, his clothes bloodstained and badly fastened. He was nursing two badly mashed fingers that still dripped blood. His face was as ravaged as that of his slave – tear-stained, pale, haggard and furious. Helen realized that he must have evaded or outrun the nuns. When he saw Helen, he cursed her and then made a fist with his undamaged hand. Helen braced herself to use the dirtiest tricks that she could remember from the days when she had to venture among rioters and terrorists. A Canadian in Pakistan had taken her in hand after she had been mugged in Quetta and taught her some moves in unarmed combat of quite unparalleled ferocity. Her carefully woven plot was already in tatters.

As he jumped forward, Laroque had to pass Jeanne. He had so far ignored the girl or had not seen her, but she was ready. She put out a foot and tripped him, and as he hit the floor Jeanne grabbed for his two broken fingers, gripped tight and twisted with the strength of her profession. Jules arrived in the doorway, ready for action, but Laroque was already helpless in agony. His cries of protest and pleas for mercy filled the house.

His key was still in the door with the other keys dangling from the ring. Helen's first move was to find the key that fitted the shackles and release the young woman. Then, under Helen's direction, Laroque was secured as the girl had been. He had regained control of his voice and continued to curse raucously, as though the impact of his hatred would be enough to subdue his attackers. The threats that he uttered increased steadily in venom.

Events were racing away in front of her, but Helen forced herself to stay calm and to think. Jeanne had strength but no experience, while Jules had never been a leader in battle whatever his strengths in business. 'Go and wash his blood off your hand,' she told Jeanne. 'Then fetch my car from the track and transfer your overnight bag from it into the Jaguar. You drive close behind me and do exactly as I do. We have a problem,' she told Jules. 'I need this man kept out of circulation for a day or two. He wasn't supposed to be on the loose but he must have evaded the nuns somehow. I want to be out of the country with the Jaguar before he's free to make trouble. In his fury, he might forget about incriminating himself.'

'I know who you are now,' Laroque hissed, 'and I swear that I will come for you some day.'

'Let's toss him into the back of my car,' Jules said. 'This offal doesn't deserve to live. I own a lot of digging machinery. A body would be no problem.' Helen was uncertain whether he was bluffing.

Laroque had fallen silent in order to listen. 'You wouldn't dare,' he said hoarsely.

Jules stirred him with his foot. 'Shut up and pray that you're a good guesser, but don't count on it.'

The young woman had dragged a coat over her nakedness. Her hair was wild. She combed it with her fingers and then tucked it behind her ears. She gave Laroque another and less gentle stir with her foot. 'Leave him to me,' she said. 'Two days? A week if you like. A month, even.' She smiled through the tear-stains. It was a smile such as Helen hoped never to see again.

'Two days will do,' said Jules. 'Then you take the Fiat and come to me. I'll draw you

267

a map. My last secretary eloped and went to Algeria, leaving most of her documents behind. You can borrow her identity. But remember, do what you like to this animal, but he must not die or I shall have to let the police know.'

'He will live,' the girl said firmly. Her face became grim. 'He may not wish to, but he will.'

'You little bitch,' Laroque raved. 'If you lay a finger on me, you will regret it until your dying day.' He turned his face towards Helen. 'As for you, keep looking over your shoulder. You'll see me coming after you.'

'The more you say,' Jules said softly, 'the more you convince me that my proposal was the better one. In common humanity I would not leave anyone else to your fate, but you are pure evil and you deserve what I am sure will come to you. You should have taken your chance with the nuns.'

Laroque fell silent.

'If anyone comes to the door, he may cry out,' said Helen to the girl.

'No one ever comes. Deliveries are left in the box at the gate; nothing is ever delivered

268

to the house. But he will not make a sound. I shall sew his mouth shut. Otherwise they would hear him in Paris when I make use of the cattle prod.' She smiled again, the smile of an imp in hell. 'But first we will have breakfast together.'

'After two days,' said Jules, 'you leave him, unchained and alive. Any longer than that and my offer of help will be withdrawn. Then you borrow the Fiat and come. I shall draw you a map.'

'I can never pay my debt to you but I will do as you say. If I still have a name, I am Monique Lefaucheaux.'

'As for you,' Helen said to Laroque, 'you'd have been better to stay where you were and face the nuns. Now you have to suffer the revenge of this woman. After that, I have friends and they will be watching you. If you ever come near this young woman or my friend here or if you ever set foot in Britain again, we will think of such things to do to you that you will never again be free from pain. Remember, it didn't take me long to find you this time, and I was not even hurrying.'

Jules and Helen walked out together. Laroque had found his voice again. The arrogant demands had given way to a mixture of threats and pleading, but they did not listen to his words. The lights of Helen's car were turning into the driveway. The garage doors were standing wide open. Helen stooped to the cockpit and checked that the E-type was out of gear before starting the engine. It muttered smoothly. According to the fuel gauge there was plenty of petrol for the night run.

She waited until the girl was settled in the driver's seat and with her seat belt fastened. They ran over the controls together. 'Follow about fifty metres behind me,' Helen said. 'I shall start slowly until you are comfortable. Do everything that I do, and if you have any problem or need to stop for any reason, flash your lights and keep flashing them.'

'I understand,' Jeanne said.

'Come and visit me, old friend,' Helen said to Jules. 'You can come and see that Jeanne is happy. There will always be a bed for you.'

He leaned close. 'An empty bed?' he whispered.

'As to that, we shall see.' She laughed under her breath. In the tension of the moment, caught between shock and relief, she wanted to howl with laughter but, she wondered, was this hysteria? 'I might break your back, had you thought of that?'

'I would risk even that.'

'Well, we shall see what we shall see.' She kissed his cheek and then turned and entered her own car. She drove to the gate and then waited. When the lights of the E-type approached, she turned towards the north and pulled slowly away. She tried to wrench her mind away from what might be happening in the house behind her.

Twenty

They drove through the remaining hours of darkness with only one halt when they ran into a belt of rain. They pulled in under the canopy of a closed filling station while they struggled to erect the E-type's soft-top. As they drove, Helen could sense the steady increase in confidence in the younger driver. As soon as they got on to the main road system, she increased speed until they were moving at or slightly over the legal limit without any sign of distress showing in the driving of the car behind. The lights of the E-type followed as though the car had been on a long trailer. After a while, they had the roads almost to themselves.

As she drove down the tunnel of her own lights, Helen's mind, tired in the let-down after the action, fell into an almost hypnotic state. Jules's parting words returned to her mind. Surely at her age physical love had to be no more than a memory. Ten years earlier, she had had a romantic encounter in Singapore, but that had been with an old flame.

Jules, of course was, in a sense, an old flame. If she now accepted his physical loving, would he be thinking of her as the nubile girl who had been on the point of surrender sixty years earlier? Would she still see him as the taut and vigorous youth? Or would they soon accept each other as altered by age but still exciting to hold? Or, the unacceptable, would each see the other as old and worn and sexless? She shook her head. Surely it was out of the question?

Yet she remembered it all so well. The glances of recognition. The touching of hands, of lips, of minds. The thrill as each barrier fell. And at last the consummation, the melting storm of pleasure followed by tranquillity.

Could one ever accept that that part of life, perhaps embodying its highest peaks, was gone forever?

They were making good time but it was a long road, made longer but faster by a detour to avoid the traffic around Paris. Helen preferred to avoid sea crossings and had decided to go back by the way that she had come. They breakfasted at Saumur and stopped at an auberge near Alençon to catch up with some sleep. They stopped again for a proper night's rest at a hotel near Amiens. Jeanne, it turned out, was exhilarated by driving the Jaguar and would have gone on, but Helen judged that the girl was close to a dangerous stage of exhaustion. They were taking breakfast at a nearby café when Helen's cellphone, which she kept charged and was carrying switched on out of habit rather than necessity, played its little tune.

Helen answered the call, expecting it to be Jules with some unforeseen disaster. Instead, David's voice came on. 'Gran, where are you?'

Jeanne leaned forward to hear the words.

'I'm on the way home.'

'That's good and it's bad. They tell me that I can go home if I have somebody to

274

look after me, but I'll be on crutches for several weeks and I'll have to keep going back for physiotherapy. I was hoping to catch you before you set off. I was going to ask you to bring Jeanne with you. Could she fly over if you sent her the fare? And would she?'

Helen and Jeanne exchanged a conspiratorial smile. Without a word, Helen handed over the phone but she kept her own ear close. In laborious English, Jeanne said, 'Your grandmother brings me with her so I shall see you soon.'

'Great! When?' David's voice was exultant.

Jeanne handed the phone back to Helen, who said, 'It depends when we can get the cars on a train through the tunnel.'

'Cars? Plural?'

'The longer we talk the later that will be. I had to bring Jeanne. I needed somebody to drive your Jaguar. I'll keep you posted.' She disconnected while David was still gabbling some question.

'That was cruel,' Jeanne said, reverting to French. 'He will be driving himself to distraction.'

'And serve him right. The lazy toad, lying in bed while we do all the work. Let's get on the road.'

They were lucky with the traffic and lucky with the trains. They were at the hospital by late afternoon. David, escorted by an anxious nurse and an occupational therapist, arrived at the front door on a pair of National Health crutches. His ankle was protected by a neat plastic shell, tidy enough to pass through a trouser leg. He was keeping his emotions in check with difficulty. He kissed his two ladies several times and looked speculatively at the two medical staff before deciding that a kiss would be inappropriate and a handshake more in keeping.

David's joy at seeing his E-type, which he had thought lost forever, was such that he wanted to travel home in it. He quite accepted that he could not work the clutch with his newly repaired ankle, but he was determined to ride as a passenger. Helen was only too well aware that he would be a terrible passenger in his own car and that his obvious unease would communicate itself to Jeanne and unsettle her to the point of danger, so she explained that the harder springing would be ruinous for his ankle and that entering and leaving the Jaguar would be close to impossible for a man with crutches. These arguments were accepted with a less-than-perfect grace and on the journey David kept screwing his head around, either to admire his car or to satisfy himself that Jeanne was not taking chances with it in the going-home traffic. Or perhaps he was enjoying a glimpse of his fiancée; Helen gave him the benefit of the tiny doubt.

'The money, I suppose, is gone beyond recall,' he said suddenly.

Helen was enjoying herself. 'It's on the back seat. Hide it tonight. You'd better pay it into the bank tomorrow morning. Or one of us will do it for you.'

'This is the night that the bank stays open late for the benefit of the night shift at Oleotech. Or have I lost track of the days?'

'You're quite right.' They caught the bank just before it closed and Helen made the unusual deposit to David's account.

None of them was dressed for dining out. Helen led Jeanne to David's door and left the pair of them while she drove home to an ecstatic greeting from her own dogs. She settled up with the house-and-dog-sitter, loaded Bigfoot the Retriever pup into her car, gathered up a random collection of edibles and returned. While David had a rapturous reunion with Bigfoot, Helen and Jeanne improvised a meal from the miscellaneous collection available. This was eaten around David's dining table in the kitchen with wine that Helen had thought to bring from home and an account of the past few days, in mixed English and French, by the two ladies, heavily censored by tacit agreement. They left David in no doubt as to the evil nature of his friend Lemaître, but glossed lightly over the fact that they had left him helpless in the power of a very vengeful young lady with a cattle prod.

'But,' said David, 'do I understand that your original plan was to have him arrested while wandering in a nunnery at night in his underpants?'

'That was it,' said his grandmother. 'A bit

of humiliation as a punishment, and a lot of publicity and a police record to hamper his future attempts at fraud. Also restitution, of course. What will drive him mad is that he paid me to break his fingers and leave him in the lurch.'

David whistled. 'You don't believe in half measures, do you? I can't think of anything more humiliating, or more certain to make every front page in France. It's a shame that it didn't come off.'

'I'd like to drink to that,' Helen said. They touched glasses. She rather thought that Monsieur Laroque might very well be in agreement by now with David's last comment. His real predicament was the greater evil. 'I wish I knew how he managed to evade a swarm of angry nuns. Either he's a high jumper of Olympic standard or there was a door that I didn't know about.'

Even the most celebratory and polyglot of parties must end. Helen was tired and stiff after the long drive and longing for her own bed. That thought begat another. Should a grandmother leave the two young people alone and unchaperoned? But she was no hypocrite. She had had enough affairs in her day, she was even still toying with the idea of yielding to Jules's approaches; and David at least must surely know something about safe sex. Let them work it out for themselves.

Despite her exhaustion, she knew where duty lay. She took her dogs for one last walk before retiring.

Twenty-one

She slept well. Her dreams were lost by morning but she sensed that they had been dreams of triumph and hope. She woke to stiffness. Her medication and painkillers did little to help. She was much too old for long drives and strange beds. A massage might help.

She took her time over dressing, feeding the dogs and taking her own breakfast. The young couple would not want to be woken early. When, from recalled experience, she reckoned that enough time had passed, she dropped her cellphone into the pouch on her belt and set off with the dogs. It was good to be back in England. She took a path between fields and through a small wood where there were bluebells still in flower and small birds sang. The dogs were in heaven, hunting among the weeds; the house-and-dog-sitter, who was terrified of losing one of her charges, had been in the habit of using the leads and sticking to paths. Helen seemed to have brought a little of the French sunshine home with her. It was going to be hot. Old bones like the heat. Global warming was not all bad news.

The door of David's cottage was slightly ajar. Without thinking, she pushed it open and walked in as she had a hundred times before. Bigfoot bounced to greet her as an old friend. Her own dogs rushed ahead, throwing open the kitchen door. Helen followed in haste, to apologize and exert control. In the kitchen David and Jeanne were seated, holding hands across a table bearing unwashed dishes. Jeanne was wearing quite the shortest nightie that Helen had ever seen. David wore only a towel round his waist.

Jeanne blushed red, lowered her eyes and tried to drag the hem of her nightdress lower, but David gave a shy grin. 'Don't be shocked, Gran,' he said. 'Try to be happy for us.'

She laughed. 'I'm not shocked,' she said. 'I know that such things happen. If I didn't know the facts of life, you wouldn't be here. Only seconds after you two met, I knew that it would happen. I just didn't think that it would happen so quickly. In my old-fashioned way I had rather hoped that marriage would precede it.'

David got up, kissed her cheek and sat down again. 'Marriage will certainly follow,' he said. 'Will that do?'

'I suppose...'

She was going to say that she supposed that that would be all that could be hoped for, but she was interrupted by the shrill sound of her mobile phone. Absently, she took it out and keyed it. She was more interested in assuring the pair of her delight in their happiness. Her attention was grabbed when she heard Jules's voice, clearly upset and gabbling in French. 'Hélène, we have trouble. Monique did not arrive. So this morning I drove back to the house of that man. The door was open, his Audi had gone and inside I found Monique's body.

283

God knows how he gained the ascendancy; it must have been while she was keeping her promise to me and releasing him, but the body already was cold. After you departed, it seemed that his hatred was focused on you, so I called to warn you. I think that you should call the police. I have already done so.'

His words had the impact of a hammer, just when she had thought that all her troubles were over. Tension was like a clamp around her forehead, putting a brake on thought. 'Thank you, Jules,' she said dully. 'I shall do that.' She disconnected and keyed for the emergency services. A great tiredness was creeping over her and there was an ache in her chest, but this was not the time to give in to her old problem. She felt in her pocket, but she had come out without her nitrolingual spray.

'Gran, what's up?'

Explaining would have taken too much time and effort. 'Listen and you'll soon know.'

Emergency services answered. She asked for the police and a brisk female voice came on the line. Her voice was not quite steady as she gave her name and address. 'But I'm at my grandson's house at the moment. That's Gabriel Cottage. I was in France recently and I made an enemy. He is highly unstable. I have just had a phone call from France to say that the man has killed his girlfriend and it is believed that he intends to come after me. He may already be in Britain. I understand that the French police have been informed.' She paused. She felt nauseous and her bowels were loose.

The voice informed her that a car was already on the way. 'Are you alone?' it asked.

'My grandson and his fiancée are here. But they know nothing of this and my grandson has one leg in a cast.'

The voice asked for more details. Her mind was too tired to think. There was too much not to say. Her first stumbling words were interrupted. There were footsteps in the passage. 'Hold on,' she said. 'There's somebody here now. I … think … it's … him.'

Without breaking the connection, she put the phone down behind her on the draining board. As she did so, she noticed that

David's largest kitchen knife was in the sink. She had time to think what an idiot she would look if it was the postman who entered. Numbness had started to spread down her left arm and the ache in her chest had become pain.

Laroque appeared in the doorway. His face was drawn with pain and disfigured by a grimace of fury. His chin was wet and around his mouth was a row of red punctures, suggesting that the young woman had indeed sewn his mouth shut. He was crumpled and unshaven. A smell followed him. Helen was surprised that any airline would let him aboard a plane or any firm hire him a car. His right hand was clumsily bandaged until it looked like a white boxing glove, but he held a chef's knife in the other hand. That, she realized, would be the most lethal weapon that a foreigner coming off a plane could purchase in a hurry.

Laroque looked from one to the other and managed a twisted smile. Three people whom he could blame for his ruin were gathered. 'So,' he said in French. 'I have you all. I shall enjoy killing you. I shall enjoy it very much.'

'The police are on the way,' Helen said. The telephone line was still open. She hoped that the call was being recorded. The dogs had begun to sense something amiss. One began growled, another barked, but they were not of fighting breeds and they had been trained that humans were never to be attacked.

Laroque raised his voice. 'They will not be here in time. You, old woman, you are the one who ruined me. Thanks to you I have killed the girl and her body is in my house and I can not return there...'

Behind her back, Helen could hear the voice of the operator demanding answers.

David and Jeanne began to get up and Helen shouted at them not to move. Jeanne saw Laroque's knife for the first time. She screamed.

It was enough. Laroque's eyes were drawn away. Helen grabbed up the knife from the sink. She used her right hand because the cardiac infarction was moving faster than ever before and her left was already useless. The pain was crucifying, but she remembered how she had dealt with the German in the barn, all those years ago. What had worked then would work again. She drove the knife up under his ribs. He looked at her for a moment, understanding slowly, then slashed with the other knife as his knees folded. She felt the bite of it but it glanced off a rib. Blackness was approaching. It would be good to sleep.

If paramedics arrived in time they might be able to pluck her out of the jaws of death, but they would have to be quick. On the whole, she thought that it was not important. She had had a great life, but it had gone on long enough. She had no regrets.